Charles Belford

Illustrated Poetry and Song

Being Selections from the best English and American Poets

Charles Belford

Illustrated Poetry and Song
Being Selections from the best English and American Poets

ISBN/EAN: 9783744768207

Printed in Europe, USA, Canada, Australia, Japan

Cover: Foto ©Andreas Hilbeck / pixelio.de

More available books at **www.hansebooks.com**

WALTER. J. ALLEN del   D.P.T. TAYLOR.

ILLUSTRATED
POETRY AND SONG

— BEING —

SELECTIONS FROM THE

BEST ENGLISH AND AMERICAN POETS,

EDITED BY

CHARLES BELFORD.

With Forty Full Page Illustrations by Dalziel, Lumley, McIntyre, Cutts,
and others.

CHICAGO:
BELFORD, CLARKE & CO.
1882.

Printed and Bound by Donahue & Henneberry.

Electrotyped By Blomgren Bros. & Co. Chicago.

LIST OF ILLUSTRATIONS

CONTENTS

CONTENTS.

CONTENTS.

CONTENTS.

LA BELLE AMERICAINE.

LA BELLE AMERICAINE.

'T is very sweet to sit and gaze, dear girl,
  On thy fair face,
As glowing as a crimson-shaded pearl
  Or lighted vase.
Young beauty brightens, like an Eden-
    dream,
  On thy pure cheek,
And joy and love from every feature seem
  To breathe and speak.

I love to kneel in worship to the Sprite
  In thy dark eyes,
Dark as the fabled Stygian stream, and
    bright
  As Paradise.
Not oft the radiance of such eyes is given
  To light our way;
And oh, to me there's not a star in heaven
  So bright as they.

I've known thee but a few brief days, and
    yet
  Thou wilt remain
An image of undying beauty, set
  On heart and brain.
Each thought, each dream of thee, fair girl,
    will seem
  Mid toil and strife,
A pure white lily swaying on the stream
  Of this dark life.

The months will pass, the flowers will soon
    be bright
  On plain and hill,
And the young birds, with voices of delight,
  The woodlands fill;
Oh, in that fairy season thou shalt be—
  'Mid budding bowers—
My heart's young May-queen, and I'll twine
    for thee
  The Heart's wild flowers.

GEO. D. PRENTICE.

SONG OF THE BROOK.

I come from haunts of coot and hern:
  I make a sudden sally
And sparkle out among the fern,
  To bicker down a valley.

By thirty hills I hurry down,
  Or slip between the ridges;
By twenty thorps, a little town,
  And half a hundred bridges.

Till last by Philip's farm I flow
  To join the brimming river:
For men may come and men may go,
  But I go on forever.

(17)

I chatter over stony ways,
  In little sharps and trebles:
I bubble into eddying bays,
  I babble on the pebbles.

With many a curve my banks I fret
  By many a field and fallow,
And many a fairy foreland set
  With willow-weed and mallow.

I chatter, chatter, as I flow
  To join the brimming river;
For men may come and men may go,
  But I go on for ever.

I wind about, and in and out,
  With here a blossom sailing,
And here and there a lusty trout,
  And here and there a grayling,

And here and there a foamy flake
  Upon me, as I travel,
With many a silvery waterbreak
  Above the golden gravel;

And draw them all along, and flow
  To join the brimming river;
For men may come and men may go,
  But I go on for ever.

I steal by lawns and grassy plots;
  I slide by hazel covers;
I move the sweet forget-me-nots
  That grow for happy lovers.

I slip, I slide, I gloom, I glance,
  Among my skimming swallows,
I make the netted sunbeam dance
  Against my sandy shallows.

I murmer under moon and stars
  In brambly wildernesses;
I linger by my shingly bars;
  I loiter round my cresses;

And out again I curve and flow
  To join the brimming river;
For men may come and men may go,
  But I go on for ever.
                    ALFRED TENNYSON.

TO VIOLETS.

WELCOME, maids of honor,
    You do bring
    In the Spring,
And wait upon her.

She has virgins many,
  · Fresh and fair;
    Yet you are
More sweet than any.

Y' are the Maiden Posies,
    And so graced,
    To be placed,
'Fore damask roses.

Yet though thus respected,
    By and by
    Ye do lie,
Poor girls, neglected.
            ROBERT HERRICK.

TO BLOSSOMS.

FAIR pledges of a fruitful tree,
    Why do ye fall so fast?
    Your date is not so past
But you may stay yet here awhile
    To blush and gently smile,
        And go at last.

What! were ye born to be
    An hour or half's delight,
    And so to bid good-night?
'Tis pity Nature brought ye forth,
    Merely to show your worth,
        And lose you quite.

But you are lovely leaves, where we
    May read how soon things have
    Their end, though ne'er so brave;
And, after they have shown their pride
    Like you awhile, they glide,
        Into the grave.
            ROBERT HERRICK.

ON THE GRASSHOPPER AND CRICKET.

THE poetry of earth is never dead:
When all the birds are faint with the hot
　　　sun
And hide in cooling trees, a voice will run
From hedge to hedge among the new-
　　mown mead.
That is the grasshopper's—he takes the
　　lead
In summer luxury,—he has never done
With his delights; for, when tired out
　　with fun,
He rests at ease beneath some pleasant
　　weed.
The poetry of earth is ceasing never.
On a lone winter evening, when the frost
Has wrought a silence, from the stove
　　there shrills
The Cricket's song in warmth increas-
　　ing ever,
And seems, to one in drowsiness half lost,
The Grasshopper's among some grassy
　　hills.

　　　　　　　　　JOHN KEATS.

LULLABY.

SWEET and low, sweet and low,
　Wind of the western sea,
Low, low, breathe and blow,
　Wind of the western sea!
Over the rolling waters go;
Come from the dying moon and blow,
　Blow him again to me;
While my little one, while my pretty
　one, sleeps.

Sleep and rest, sleep and rest;
　Father will come to thee soon.
Rest, rest on mother's breast;
　Father will come to thee soon.
Father will come to his babe in the nest;
Silver sails all out of the west
　Under the silver moon;
Sleep, my little one, sleep, my pretty one,
　sleep.

　　　　　　　　ALFRED TENNYSON.

CHILDREN.

CHILDREN are what the mothers are.
No fondest father's fondest care
Can fashion so the infant heart
As those creative beams that dart,
With all their hopes and fears, upon
The cradle of a sleeping son.

His startled eyes with wonder see
A father near him on his knee,
Who wishes all the while to trace
The mother in his future face;
But 't is to her alone uprise
His wakening arms; to her those eyes
Open with joy and not surprise.

　　　　　　WALTER SAVAGE LANDOR.

A RECEIPT FOR SALAD.

To make this condiment your poet begs
The pounded yellow of two hard-boiled
　　eggs;
Two boiled potatoes, passed through kitch-
　　en sieve,
Smoothness and softness to the salad give;
Let onion atoms lurk within the bowl,
And, half suspected, animate the whole;
Of mordent mustard add a single spoon,
Distrust the condiment that bites too soon;
But deem it not, thou man of herbs, a fault
To add a double quantity of salt;
Four times the spoon with oil from Lucca
　　crown,
And twice with vinegar, procured from
　　town;
And lastly, o'er the flavored compound toss
A magic soupcon of anchovy sauce.
Oh, green and glorious! Oh, herbaceous
　　treat!
'Twould tempt the dying anchorite to eat;
Back to the world he'd turn his fleeting soul,
And plunge his fingers in the salad bowl;
Serenely full, the epicure would say,
"Fate cannot harm me,—I have dined
　　to-day."

　　　　　　　　SYDNEY SMITH.

THE USEFUL PLOW.

A country life is sweet,
In moderate cold and heat,
To walk in the air how pleasant and fair!
In every field of wheat,
The fairest of flowers adorning the bowers,
And every meadow's brow;
So that, I say, no courtier may
Compare with them who clothe in gray,
And follow the useful plow.

They rise with the morning lark,
And labor till almost dark,
Then, folding their sheep, they hasten to
sleep,
While every pleasant park
Next morning is ringing with the birds
that are singing
On each green, tender bough.
With what content and merriment
Their days are spent, whose minds are bent
To follow the useful plow!

ANONYMOUS.

TAKE, OH! TAKE THOSE LIPS AWAY.

TAKE, oh! take those lips away
That so sweetly were forsworn,
And those eyes, the break of day,
Lights that do mislead the morn!
But my kisses bring again,
Seals of love, though sealed in vain.

Hide, oh! hide those hills of snow
Which thy frozen bosom bears,
On whose tops the pinks that grow
Are of those that April wears.
But first set my poor heart free,
Bound in those icy chains by thee.

SHAKESPEARE and JOHN FLETCHER.

SONNETS

ON HIS BEING ARRIVED TO THE AGE OF TWENTY-THREE.

How soon hath time, the subtle thief of
youth,
Stolen on his wing my three and twen-
tieth year!
My hasting days fly on with full career,
But my late spring no bud or blossom
showeth.
Perhaps my semblance might deceive the
truth,
That I to manhood am arrived so near:
And inward ripeness doth much less
appear
That some more timely-happy spirits in-
du'th.
Yet be it less or more, or soon or slow,
It shall be still in strictest measure even
To that same lot, however mean or high,
Toward which time leads me, and the will
of heaven:
All is, if I have grace to use it so,
As ever in my great task-master's eye.

JOHN MILTON.

AULD LANG SYNE.

I.

SHOULD auld acquaintance be forgot,
And never brought to min'?
Should auld acquaintance be forgot,
And days o' lang syne?
For auld lang syne, my dear,
For auld lang syne,
We'll tak a cup o' kindness yet
For auld lang syne!

II

We twa hae run about the braes,
And pu'd the gowans fine;
But we've wandered mony a weary foot
Sin auld lang syne.

THE USEFUL PLOW.

III.

We twa hae paidl't i' the burn
  Frae mornin' sun till dine;
But seas between us braid hae roared
  Sin auld lang syne.

IV.

And here's a hand, my trusty fiere,
  And gie's a hand o' thine;
And we'll take a right guid wille-waught
  For auld lang syne!

V.

And surely ye'll be your pint-stowp,
  And surely I'll be mine:
And we'll take a cup o' kindness yet
  For auld lang syne.
For auld lang syne, my dear,
  For auld lang syne,
We'll tak a cup o' kindness yet,
  For auld lang syne!

ROBERT BURNS.

SPRING.

Now the lusty Spring is seen;
  Golden yellow, gaudy blue,
  Daintily invite the view.
Everywhere, on every green,
Roses blushing as they blow,
  And enticing men to pull;
Lilies whiter than the snow;
Woodbines of sweet honey full—
  All love's emblems, and all cry:
  Ladies, if not plucked, we die!

BEAUMONT AND FLETCHER.

SOFTLY WOO AWAY HER BREATH.

SOFTLY woo away her breath,
  Gentle death!
Let her leave thee with no strife,
  Tender, mournful, murmering life!

She hath seen her happy day—
  She hath had her bud and blossom;
Now she pales and shrinks away,
  Earth, into thy gentle bosom!

She hath done her bidding here,
  Angels dear!
Bear her perfect soul above,
  Seraph of the skies—sweet love!
Good she was, and fair in youth;
  And her mind was seen to soar,
And her heart was wed to truth:
  Take her, then, for evermore—
For ever—evermore!

BARRY CORNWALL.

THE MAY QUEEN.

I.

You must wake and call me early, call me
    early, mother dear;
To-morrow'll be the happiest time of all
    the glad new-year—
Of all the glad new-year, mother, the mad-
    dest, merriest day;
For I'm to be queen o' the May, mother,
    I'm to be queen o' the May.

II.

There's many a black, black eye, they say,
    but none so bright as mine;
There's Margaret and Mary, there's Kate
    and Caroline;
But none so fair as little Alice in all the
    land, they say;
So I'm to be queen o' the May, mother,
    I'm to be queen o' the May.

III.

I sleep so sound all night, mother, that I
    shall never wake,
If you do not call me loud, when the day
    begins to break;
But I must gather knots of flowers and
    buds, and garlands gay;
For I'm to be queen o' the May, mother,
    I'm to be queen o' the May.

IV.

As I came up the valley, whom think ye
   should I see,
But Robin leaning on the bridge beneath
   the hazel-tree?
He thought of that sharp look, mother, I
   gave him yesterday,—
But I'm to be queen o' the May, mother,
   I'm to be queen o' the May.

V.

He thought I was a ghost, mother, for I
   was all in white;
And I ran by him without speaking, like a
   flash of light.
They call me cruel-hearted, but I care not
   what they say,
For I'm to be queen o' the May, mother,
   I'm to be queen o' the May.

VI.

They say he's dying all for love—but that
   can never be;
They say his heart is breaking, mother—
   what is that to me?
There's many a bolder lad'll woo me any
   summer day;
And I'm to be queen o' the May, mother,
   I'm to be queen o' the May.

VII.

Little Effie shall go with me to-morrow to
   the green,
And you'll be there, too, mother, to see me
   made the queen;
For the shepherd lads on every side'll come
   from far away;
And I'm to be queen o' the May, mother,
   I'm to be queen o' the May.

VIII.

The honeysuckle round the porch has
   woven its wavy bowers,
And by the meadow-trenches blow the
   faint sweet cuckoo-flowers;
And the wild marsh-marigold shines like
   fire in swamps and hollows gray;
And I'm to be queen o' the May, mother,
   I'm to be queen o' the May.

IX.

The night-winds come and go, mother,
   upon the meadow-grass,
And the happy stars above them seem to
   brighten as they pass;
There will not be a drop of rain the whole
   of the livelong day;
And I'm to be queen o' the May, mother,
   I'm to be queen o' the May.

X.

All the valley, mother, 'll be fresh and green
   and still,
And the cowslip and the crowfoot are over
   all the hill.
And the rivulet in the flowery dale 'll mer-
   rily glance and play,
For I'm to be queen o' the May, mother,
   I'm to be queen o' the May.

XI.

So you must wake and call me early, call
   me early, mother dear,
To-morrow 'll be the happiest time of all
   the glad new-year:
To-morrow 'll be of all the year the mad-
   dest, merriest day,
For I'm to be queen o' the May, mother,
   I'm to be queen o' the May.

NEW YEAR'S EVE.

I.

If you're waking, call me early, call me
   early, mother dear,
For I would see the sun rise upon the glad
   new-year.
It is the last new year that I shall ever see—
Then you may lay me low i' the mould,
   and think no more of me.

II.

To-night I saw the sun set—he set and
   left behind
The good old year, the dear old time, and
   all my peace of mind;

And the new year's coming up, mother;
but I shall never see
The blossom on the blackthorn, the leaf
upon the tree.

III.

Last May we made a crown of flowers;
we had a merry day—
Beneath the hawthorn on the green they
made me queen of May;
And we danced about the May-pole and
in the hazel copse,
Till Charles's Wain came out above the
tall white chimney-tops.

IV.

There's not a flower on all the hills—the
frost is on the pane;
I only wish to live till the snowdrops come
again.
I wish the snow would melt and the sun
come out on high—
I long to see a flower so before the day I
die.

V.

The building rook 'll craw from the windy
tall elm tree,
And the tufted plover pipe along the fallow
lea,
And the swallow 'll come back again with
summer o'er the wave,
But I shall lie alone, mother, within the
mouldering grave.

VI.

Upon the chancel-casement, and upon that
grave of mine,
In the early, early morning the summer
sun 'll shine,
Before the red cock crows from the farm
upon the hill—
When you are warm-asleep, mother, and
all the world is still.

VII.

When the flowers come again, mother, beneath the waning light
You 'll never see me more in the long gray
fields at night;

When from the dry dark wold the summer
airs blow cool
On the oat-grass and the sword-grass, and
the bulrush in the pool.

VIII.

You 'll bury me, my mother, just beneath
the hawthorn shade,
And you 'll come sometimes and see me
where I am lowly laid.
I shall not forget you, mother; I shall
hear you when you pass,
With your feet above my head in the long
and pleasant grass.

IX.

I have been wild and wayward, but you'll
forgive me now;
You 'll kiss me, my own mother, upon my
cheek and brow;
Nay, nay, you must not weep, nor let your
grief be wild;
You should not fret for me, mother,—
you have another child.

X.

If I can, I 'll come again, mother, from out
my resting place;
Though you 'll not see me mother, I shall
look upon your face;
Though I cannot speak a word, I shall
hearken what you say,
And be often, often with. you when you
think I'm far away.

XI.

Good-night! good-night! when I have said
good-night for evermore,
And you see me carried out from the
threshold of the door,
Don't let Effie come to see me till my
grave be growing green—
She 'll be a better child to you than ever I
have been.

XII.

She 'll find my garden tools upon the granary floor.
Let her take 'em—they are hers; I shall
never garden more.

But tell her, when I'm gone, to train the
  rose-bush that I set
About the parlor window, and the box of
  mignonette.

XIII.

Good-night, sweet mother! Call me before the day is born.
All night I lie awake, but I fall asleep at
  morn;
But I would see the sun rise upon the glad
  new-year—
So, if you're waking, call me, call me
  early, mother dear.

CONCLUSION.

I THOUGHT to pass away before, and yet
  alive I am;
And in the fields all round I hear the
  bleating of the lamb.
How sadly, I remember, rose the morning
  of the year!
To die before the snowdrop came, and now
  the violet's here.

II.

Oh sweet is the new violet, that comes
  beneath the skies;
And sweeter is the young lamb's voice to
  me that cannot rise;
And sweet is all the land about, and all the
  flowers that blow;
And sweeter far is death than life, to me
  that longs to go.

III.

It seemed so hard at first, mother, to leave
  the blessed sun,
And now it seems as hard to stay; and yet,
  His will be done!
But still I think it can't be long before I
  find release;
And that good man the clergyman, has
  told me words of peace.

IV.

Oh blessings on his kindly voice, and on
  his silver hair!
And blessings on his whole life long, until
  he meet me there!
Oh blessings on his kindly heart and on
  his silver head!
A thousand times I blest him, as he knelt
  beside my bed.

V.

He showed me all the mercy, for he taught
  me all the sin;
Now, though my lamp was lighted late
  there's One will let me in.
Nor would I now be well, mother, again, if
  that could be;
For my desire is but to pass to Him that
  died for me.

VI.

I did not hear the dog howl, mother, or the
  · death-watch beat—
There came a sweeter token when the
  night and morning meet;
But sit beside my bed, mother, and put your
  hand in mine,
And Effie on the other side, and I will tell
  the sign.

VII.

All in the wild March-morning I heard
  the angels call—
It was when the moon was setting, and the
  dark was over all;
The trees began to whisper, and the wind
  began to roll,
And in the wild March-morning I heard
  them call my soul.

VIII.

For lying broad awake, I thought of you
  and Effie dear;
I saw you sitting in the house, and I no
  longer here;
With all my strength I prayed for both—
  and so I felt resigned,
And up the valley came a swell of music
  · on the wind.

IX.

I thought that it was fancy, and I listened
in my bed;
And then did something speak to me—I
know not what was said;
For great delight and shuddering took hold
of all my mind,
And up the valley came again the music
on the wind.

X.

But you were sleeping; and I said, "It's
not for them—it's mine;"
And if it comes three times, I thought, I
take it for a sign.
And once again it came, and close beside
the window-bars—
Then seemed to go right up to heaven and
die among the stars.

XI.

So now I think my time is near; I trust it
is. I know
The blessed music went that way my soul
will have to go.
And for myself, indeed, I care not if I go
to-day;
But Effie, you must comfort her when I
am past away.

XII.

And say to Robin a kind word, and tell
him not to fret;
There's many worthier than I would make
him happy yet.
If I had lived—I cannot tell—I might have
been his wife;
But all these things have ceased to be, with
my desire of life.

XIII.

Oh look! the sun begins to rise! the heavens are in a glow;
He shines upon a hundred fields, and all of
them I know.
And there I move no longer now, and
there his light may shine—
Wild flowers in the valley for other hands
than mine.

XIV.

Oh sweet and strange it seems to me, that
ere this day is done
The voice that now is speaking may be beyond the sun—
For ever and for ever with those just souls
and true—
And what is life, that we should moan?
why make we such ado?

XV.

For ever and for ever, all in a blessed home,
And there to wait a little while till you and
Effie come—
To lie within the light of God, as I lie upon
your breast—
And the wicked cease from troubling, and
the weary are at rest.

ALFRED TENNYSON.

I REMEMBER, I REMEMBER.

I REMEMBER, I remember
The house where I was born,
The little window where the sun
Came peeping in at morn;
He never came a wink too soon,
Nor brought too long a day;
But now, I often wished the night
Had borne my breath away!

I remember, I remember
The roses, red and white,
The violets, and the lily-cups—
Those flowers made of light!
The lilacs where the robin built,
And where my brother set
The laburnum on his birthday,—
The tree is living yet!

I remember, I remember
Where I was used to swing,
And thought the air must rush as fresh
To swallows on the wing;
My spirit flew in feathers then,
That is so heavy now,
And summer pools could hardly cool
The fever on my brow!

I remember, I remember
The fir-trees dark and high;
I used to think their slender tops
Were close against the sky.
It was a childish ignorance,
But now 't is little joy
To know I'm farther off from Heaven
Than when I was a boy.

THOMAS HOOD.

TO THE EVENING STAR.

STAR that bringest home the bee,
And sett'st the weary laborer free!
If any star shed peace, 't is thou,
That send'st it from above,
Appearing when Heaven's breath and brow
Are sweet as hers we love.

Come to the luxuriant skies,
Whilst the landscape's odors rise,
Whilst, far off, lowing herds are heard,
And songs when toil is done,
From cottages whose smoke unstirred
Curls yellow in the sun.

Star of love's soft interviews,
Parted lovers on thee muse;
Their remembrancer in Heaven
Of thrilling vows thou art,
Too delicious to be riven,
By absence, from the heart.

THOMAS CAMPBELL.

MY VALENTINE.

How, prithee, shall I woo my Love—
My Valentine?
By MISSIVE sweet
And scented as the airs that rove
Around her bow'r
At evening hour,
And vie in haste to kiss her feet;

Or with FOND HOPES—
As rosy-hued
As my Celia's damask cheek—
When with blushes scarce subdued
In maiden pride
She turns aside
Whene'er my love I would outspeak!

With RICHES—
Golden as her hair
Where envious sunbeams frequent play,
Tho' fain, uncertain to rest where
'Midst locks so bright
Their borrow'd light
Must die, or living pass away!

Or woo her with a CORONET—
Rare jewels,
Bright as her pure eyes,
Which peep beneath their lashes wet,
In coyest fear
Lest love appear
To claim their glances for his prize.

Or suppliant, her PITY move
With tears for my forlorn estate;
Such pity near akin to love.
Ah, happy swain,
Would she but deign
With my unworthiness to mate!

No! None of these will I address
To her, my true-lov'd Valentine!
But with a longing tenderness
I'll seek her bow'r,
At twilight hour,
And boldly claim to call her mine!

There my LOVE alone I'll plead,
While Faith and Truth shall witness bear,
For Honors, Riches, I've no need,
By Cupid arm'd
I'll rise unharmed
From stubborn conflict with despair.

And tho' no word to me she say,
I'll know by one sweet, tender sign
That she forever, day by day,
Thro' good and ill
Will love me still,
My own true-hearted Valentine!

H. FRITH.

COMING THROUGH THE RYE.

Gin a body meet a body
  Comin' through the rye,
Gin a body kiss a body,
  Need a body cry?
Every lassie has her laddie—
  Ne'er a ane hae I;
Yet a' the lads they smile at me
  When comin' through the rye.
Amang the train there is a swain
  I dearly lo'e mysel';
But whaur his hame, or what his name,
  I dinna care to tell.

Gin a body meet a body
  Comin' frae the town,
Gin a body greet a body,
  Need a body frown?
Every lassie has her laddie—
  Ne'er a ane hae I;
Yet a' the lads they smile at me
  When comin' through the rye.
Amang the train there is a swain
  I dearly lo'e mysel';
But whaur his hame, or what his name,
  I dinna care to tell.

ANONYMOUS.

FAIRY SONG.

Shed no tear! oh shed no tear!
The flower will bloom another year.
Weep no more! oh weep no more!
Young buds sleep in the root's white core,
Dry your eyes! oh dry your eyes!
For I was taught in Paradise
To ease my breast of melodies—
        Shed no tear.

Overhead! look overhead!
'Mong the blossoms white and red—
Look up! look up! I flutter now
On this fresh pomegranate bough
See me! 't is this silvery bill
Ever cures the good man's ill.
Shed no tear! oh shed no tear!
The flower will bloom another year.
Adieu, adieu—I fly—adieu!
I vanish in the heaven's blue—
        Adieu, adieu!

JOHN KEATS.

THE HARP THAT ONCE THROUGH TARA'S HALLS.

The harp that once through Tara's halls
  The soul of music shed,
Now hangs as mute on Tara's walls,
  As if that soul were fled.
So sleeps the pride of former days,
  So glory's thrill is o'er,
And hearts that once beat high for praise, .
  Now feel that pulse no more.

No more to chiefs and ladies bright
  The harp of Tara swells;
The chord alone that breaks at night
  Its tale of ruin tells.
Thus freedom now so seldom wakes,
  The only throb she gives
Is when some heart indignant breaks
  To show that still she lives.

THOMAS MOORE.

AN ELEGY ON THE DEATH OF A MAD DOG.

Good people all, of every sort,
  Give ear unto my song;
And if you find it wond'rous short
  It cannot hold you long.

In Islington there was a man,
  Of whom the world might say
That still a godly race he ran
  When e'er he went to pray.

A kind and gentle heart he had,
  To comfort friends and foes;
The naked every day he clad,
  When he put on his clothes.

And in that town a dog was found,
  As many dogs there be,
Both mongrel, puppy, whelp, and hound,
  And curs of low degree.

This dog and man at first were friends;
  But when a pique began,
The dog, to gain his private ends,
  Went mad, and bit the man.

Around from all the neighboring streets
  The wandering neighbors ran,
And swore the dog had lost his wits,
  To bite so good a man.

The wound it seemed both sore and sad
  To every Christian eye:
And while they swore the dog was mad
  They swore the man would die.

But soon a wonder came to light,
  That showed the rogues they lied:
The man recovered of the bite,
  The dog it was that died.

                    OLIVER GOLDSMITH.

"PROUD MAISIE IS IN THE WOOD."

PROUD Maisie is in the wood,
  Walking so early;
Sweet robin sits on the bush
  Singing so rarely.

"Tell me, thou bonny bird,
  When shall I marry me?"
—"When six braw gentlemen
  Kirkward shall carry ye."

"Who makes the bridal bed,
  Birdie, say truly?"
—"The gray-headed sexton
  That delves the grave duly.

"The glow-worm o'er grave and stone
  Shall light thee steady;
The owl from the steeple sing
  Welcome, proud lady!"

                    SIR WALTER SCOTT.

THE WISHING-WELL.

WHAT! you are come, despite your boast
  You are not superstitious?
No faith in fairies, nor in ghosts,
  Nor Wishing-Well? Delicious

I know you better, and I hide
  Within the hollow oak;
To the clear spring your wish confide—
  Nor spring, nor I, will joke.

I see you've culled the small blue flower
  I told you of last night;
You come, too, at the sunset hour,
  Determined to be right.

You fix your eyes upon the ground,
  Are counting nine times nine;
My mysteries your thoughts have bound—
  Approach, sweet Geraldine.

There, now upon the steps you stand,
  You gaze upon the wave,
The flowers poised within your hand,
  Why, Geraldine, how grave!

You lightly laughed at all I said
  About the mystic spell,
And thrice you shook your pretty head
  Against the Wishing-Well.

Some stronger faith enthrals you now,
  Your mirth owns some eclipse;
A shade of thought is on your brow,
  No smile upon your lips.

Your face reflected there you trace,
  And, by some fancy's freak,
As you gaze down upon your face
  The waters seem to speak.

"Hail! fairest form of womanhood
  That we have ever pressed
On summer eve, amid the wood,
  Upon our peaceful breast.

"For many a maid has lingered here,
  And all her secrets told,
And troubled us with lying tear,
  While wishing but for gold.

"And gallant youths from town and hall
  Have given us their trust:
But, ah! their love was hollow all,
  Another name for lust.

"We grant no wish that is not pure,
  No hope for selfish gain;
We love no love that can't endure—
  No pleasure void of pain.

"And now thrice welcome we bid you;
  We know the sacred sign
That marks a maiden pure and true,
  As you are Geraldine!

THE WISHING WELL.

" So drop the flower from your hand,
  We hold it fondly given;
Pause but one moment on the strand,
  And breathe your wish to Heaven."

The flower falls! the Well receives
  Your gift—and, also, mine;
No withered buds; no Autumn leaves—
  Bright blossoms, Geraldine.

I hold your hand—to hold your heart
  Soon in the marriage spell;
And thus we vow no more to part,
  Beside the Wishing-Well!

CHARLES LAURENCE YOUNG.

BARBARA FRIETCHIE.

Up from the meadows rich with corn,
Clear in the cool September morn,

The clustered spires of Frederick stand
Green-walled by the hills of Maryland.

Round about them orchards sweep,
Apple and peach-tree fruited deep,

Fair as a garden of the Lord
To the eyes of the famished rebel horde;

On that pleasant morn of the early fall
When Lee marched over the mountain wall,

Over the mountains, winding down,
Horse and foot into Frederick town.

Forty flags with their silver stars,
Forty flags with their crimson bars,

Flapped in the morning wind; the sun
Of noon looked down, and saw not one.

Up rose old Barbara Frietchie then,
Bowed with her fourscore years and ten;

Bravest of all in Frederick town,
She took up the flag the men hauled down;

In her attic-window the staff she set,
To show that one heart was loyal yet.

Up the street came the rebel tread,
Stonewall Jackson riding ahead.

Under his slouched hat left and right
He glanced: the old flag met his sight.

" Halt!"—the dust-brown ranks stood fast;
" Fire!"—out blazed the rifle-blast

It shivered the window, pane and sash,
It rent the banner with seam and gash.

Quick, as it fell, from the broken staff
Dame Barbara snatched the silken scarf;

She leaned far out on the window-sill,
And shook it forth with a royal will.

" Shoot, if you must, this old grey head,
But spare your country's flag," she said.

A shade of sadness, a blush of shame,
Over the face of the leader came;

The nobler nature within him stirred
To life at that woman's deed and word:

" Who touches a hair of yon grey head
Dies like a dog! March on!" he said.

All day long through Frederick street
Sounded the tread of marching feet·

All day long that free flag tost
Over the heads of the rebel host.

Ever its torn folds rose and fell
On the loyal winds that loved it well;

And through the hill-gaps sunset light
Shone over it with a warm good-night.

Barbara Frietchie's work is o'er,
And the rebel rides on his raids no more.

Honor to her! and let a tear
Fall, for her sake, on Stonewall's bier.

Over Barbara Frietchie's grave,
Flag of freedom and union, wave!

Peace, and order, and beauty draw
Round thy symbol of light and law;

And ever the stars above look down
On thy stars below in Frederick town!

JOHN GREENLEAF WHITTIER.

A DOUBTING HEART.

WHERE are the swallows fled?
    Frozen and dead
Perchance upon some bleak and stormy
        shore
    O doubting heart!
    Far over purple seas,
    They wait, in sunny ease,
    The balmy southern breeze
To bring them to their northern homes
       once more.

Why must the flowers die?
    Prisoned they lie
In the cold tomb, heedless of tears or rain.
    O doubting heart!
    They only sleep below
    The soft white ermine snow
    While winter winds shall blow,
To breathe and smile upon you soon again.

The sun has hid its rays
    These many days;
Will dreary hours never leave the earth?
    O doubting heart!
    The stormy clouds on high
    Veil the same sunny sky
    That soon, for spring is nigh,
Shall wake the Summer into golden mirth.

Fair hope is dead, and light
    Is quenched in night;
What sound can break the silence of despair?
    O doubting heart!
    The sky is overcast,
    Yet stars shall rise at last,
    Brighter for darkness past,
And angels' silver voices stir the air.

        ADELAIDE ANNE PROCTER.

———

"WHEN THE HOUNDS OF SPRING."

WHEN the hounds of spring are on winter's
    traces,
    The mother of months in meadow or plain
Fills the shadows and windy places
    With lisp of leaves and ripple of rain;

And the brown bright nightingale amorous
Is half assuaged for Itylus,
For the Thracian ships and the foreign faces;
    The tongueless vigil, and all the pain.

Come with bows bent and with emptying
    of quivers,
    Maiden most perfect, lady of light,
With a noise of winds and many rivers,
    With a clamor of waters, and with might;
Bind on thy sandals, O thou most fleet,
Over the splendor and speed of thy feet!
For the faint east quickens, the wan west
    shivers,
    Round the feet of the day and the feet of
    the night.

Where shall we find her, how shall we sing
    to her,
    Fold our hands round her knees and
    cling?
Oh that man's heart were as fire and could
    spring to her,
    Fire, or the strength of the streams that
    spring!
For the stars and the winds are unto her
As raiment, as songs of the harp-player;
For the risen stars and the fallen cling to her,
    And the south-west wind and the west
    wind sing.

For winter's rains and ruins are over,
    And all the season of snows and sins;
The days dividing lover and lover,
    The light that loses, the night that wins;
And time remembered is grief forgotten,
And frosts are slain and flowers begotten,
And in green underwood and cover
    Blossom by blossom the spring begins.

The full streams feed on flower of rushes,
    Ripe grasses trammel a travelling foot,
The faint fresh flame of the young year
    flushes
    From leaf to flower and flower to fruit;
And fruit and leaf are as gold and fire,
And the oat is heard above the lyre,
And the hoofed heel of a satyr crushes
    The chestnut-husk at the chestnut-root.

And Pan by noon and Bacchus by night,
Fleeter of foot than the fleet-foot kid,
Follows with dancing and fills with delight
The Mænad and Bassarid;
And soft as lips that laugh and hide,
The laughing leaves of the trees divide,
And screen from seeing and leave in sight
The god pursuing, the maiden hid.

The ivy falls with the Bacchanal's hair
Over her eyebrows shading her eyes;
The wild vine slipping down leaves bare
Her bright breast shortening into sighs;
The wild vine slips with the weight of its
leaves,
But the berried ivy catches and cleaves
To the limbs that glitter, the feet that scare
The wolf that follows, the fawn that flies.
ALGERNON CHARLES SWINBURNE.

MY HEART'S IN THE HIGHLANDS.

My heart 's in the Highlands, my heart is
not here;
My heart 's in the Highlands a-chasing the
deer.
Chasing the wild deer, and following the roe,
My heart 's in the Highlands wherever I go.
Farewell to the Highlands, farewell to the
North,
The birth-place of valor, the country of
worth;
Wherever I wander, wherever I rove,
The hills of the Highlands forever I love.
Farewell to the mountains high covered
with snow;
Farewell to the straths and green valleys
below;
Farewell to the forests and wild-hanging
woods;
Farewell to the torrents and loud-pouring
floods.
My heart 's in the Highlands, my heart is
not here,
My heart 's in the Highlands a-chasing the
deer;
Chasing the wild deer, and following the
roe,
My heart 's in the Highlands, wherever I go·
ROBERT BURNS.

THE HUNTER'S SONG.

RISE! Sleep no more! 'T is a noble morn.
The dews hang thick on the fringed thorn.
And the frost shrinks back, like a beaten
hound,
Under the steaming, steaming ground.
Behold, where the billowy clouds flow by,
And leave us alone in the clear gray sky!
Our horses are ready and steady.—So, ho!
I 'm gone, like a dart from a Tartar's bow.
Hark, hark!— Who calleth the maiden Morn
From her sleep in the woods and the stubble
corn?
　　　The horn,—the horn!
The merry, sweet ring of the hunter's horn.

Now, through the copse where the fox is
found,
And over the stream at a mighty bound,
And over the high lands and over the low,
O'er furrows, o'er meadows, the hunters go!
Away!—as a hawk flies full at his prey,
So flieth the hunter, away,—away!
From the burst at the cover till set of sun,
When the red fox dies, and—the day is done.
Hark, hark! — What sound on the wind is
borne?
'T is the conquering voice of the hunter's horn:
　　　The horn,—the horn!
The merry, bold voice of the hunter's horn.

Sound! Sound the horn! To the hunter
good
What 's the gully deep or the roaring flood?
Right over he bounds, as the wild stag
bounds.
At the heels of his swift, sure, silent,
hounds,
Oh, what delight can a mortal lack,
When once he is firm on his horse's back,
With his stirrups short, and his snaffle
strong,
And the blast of the horn for his morning
song?
Hark, hark!—Now, home! and dream till
morn
Of the bold, sweet sound of the hunter's horn!
　　　The horn,—the horn!
Oh, the sound of all sounds is the hunter's
horn!
BARRY CORNWALL.

AN EVENING IN SPRING

AVE MARIA! o'er the earth and sea,
That heavenliest hour of heaven is wor-
    thiest thee!

Ave Maria! blessed be the hour,
    The time, the clime, the spot, where I
    so oft
Have felt that moment in its fullest power
    Sink o'er the earth so beautiful and soft,
While swung the deep bell in the distant
    tower
Or the faint dying day-hymn stole aloft,
And not a breath crept through the rosy air,
And yet the forest leaves seemed stirred
    with prayer.

Ave Maria! 't is the hour of prayer!'
    Ave Maria! 't is the hour of love!
Ave Maria! may our spirits dare
    Look up to thine and thy Son's above!
Ave Maria! O that face so fair
    Those downcast eyes beneath the Al-
    mighty dove,—
What tHough 't is but a pictured image—
    strike,—
That painting is no idol,—'t is too like.

Sweet hour of twilight! in the solitude
    Of the pine forest, and the silent shore
Which bounds Ravenna's immemorial
    wood,
    Rooted where once the Adrian wave
    flowed o'er.
To where the last Cæsarean fortress stood,
    Evergreen forest; which Boccaccio's lore
And Dryden's lay made haunted ground to
    me,
How have I loved the twilight hour and
    thee!

The shrill cicalas, people of the pine,
    Making their summer lives one ceaseless
    song,
Were the sole echoes, save my steed's and
    mine,

And vesper-bells that rose the boughs
    along;
The spectre huntsman of Onesti's line,
    His hell-dogs, and their chase, and the
    fair throng,
Which learned from this example not to
    fly
From a true lover,—shadowed my mind's
    eye.

O Hesperus! thou bringest all good things—
    Home to the weary, to the hungry cheer,
To the young bird the parent's brooding
    wings,
    The welcome stall to the o'erlaboured
    steer;
Whate'er of peace about our hearthstone
    clings,
Whate'er our household gods protect of
    dear,
Are gathered round us by thy look of rest:
Thou bring'st the child, too, to the mother's
    breast.

Soft hour! which wakes the wish and melts
    the heart
    Of those who sail the seas, on the first
    day
When they from their sweet friends are
    torn apart;
    Or fills with love the pilgrim on his way,
(As the far bell of vesper makes him start,
    Seeming to weep the dying day's decay);
Is this a fancy which our reason scorns?
Ah! surely nothing dies but something
    mourns.   LORD BYRON.

TO AUTUMN.

SEASON of mists and mellow fruitfulness!
    Close bosom-friend of the maturing sun!
Conspiring with him how to load and bless
    With fruit the vines that round the
    thatcheaves run—
To bend with apples and mossed cottage
    trees,

AN EVENING IN SPRING.

And fill all fruit with ripeness to the core—
  To swell the gourd, and plump the hazel
    shells
With a sweet kernel—to set budding,
    more
And still more, later flowers for the bees,
Until they think warm days will never
    cease.
  For summer has o'er-brimmed their
    clammy cells.

Who hath not seen thee oft amid thy store?
  Sometimes whoever seeks abroad may
    find
Thee sitting careless on a granary floor,
  Thy hair soft-lifted by the winnowing
    wind;
Or on a half-reaped furrow sound asleep,
  Drowsed with the fume of poppies, while
    thy hook
    Spares the next swath and all its twin-
    ed flowers;
And sometime like a gleaner thou dost keep
  Steady thy laden head across a brook;
  Or by a cider-press, with patient look,
    Thou watchest the last oozings, hours
    by hours.

Where are the songs of Spring? Ay,
    where are they?
  Think not of them—thou hast thy music
    too:
While barred clouds bloom the soft-dying
    day,
  And touch the stubble-plains with rosy
    hue;
Then in a wailful choir the small gnats
    mourn
  Among the river sallows, borne aloft
    Or sinking, as the light wind lives or
    dies;
And full-grown lambs loud bleat from
    hilly bourn;
  Hedge-crickets sing; and now with treble
    soft
The red-breast whistles from the garden
    croft,
    And gathering swallows twitter in the
    skies.

                          JOHN KEATS.

AUTUMN—A DIRGE.

THE warm sun is failing; the bleak wind
    is wailing;
The bare boughs are sighing; the pale flow-
    ers are dying;
        And the Year
On the earth, her death-bed, in shroud of
    leaves dead,
        Is lying,
    Come, months, come away,
    From November to May;
    In your saddest array
    Follow the bier
    Of the dead, cold Year,
And like dim shadows watch by her sepul-
    chre.

The chill rain is falling; the nipt worm is
    crawling;
The rivers are swelling; the thunder is
    knelling
        For the Year;
The blithe swallows are flown and the
    lizards each gone
        To his dwelling;
    Come, months, come away;
    Put on white, black, and gray;
    Let your light sisters play—
    Ye, follow the bier
    Of the dead, cold Year,
And make her grave green with tear on
    tear.

                  PERCY BYSSHE SHELLEY.

'TIS THE LAST ROSE OF SUMMER.

'TIS the last rose of Summer,
    Left blooming alone;
All her lovely companions
    Are faded and gone;
No flower of her kindred,
    No rosebud is nigh,
To reflect back her blushes,
    Or give sigh for sigh!

I'll not leave thee, thou lone one,
    To pine on the stem;
Since the lovely are sleeping,

Go sleep thou with them.
Thus kindly I scatter
. Thy leaves o'er the bed
Where thy mates of the garden
   Lie scentless and dead.

So soon may I follow,
   When friendships decay,
And from Love's shining circle
   The gems drop away!
When true hearts lie withered,
   And fond ones are flown,
Oh! who would inhabit
   This bleak world alone?
           THOMAS MOORE.

COSTUME.

I.

STILL to be neat, still to be drest,
As you were going to a feast;
Still to be powdered, still to be perfumed,—
Lady, it is to be presumed,
Though art's hid causes are not found,
All is not sweet, all is not sound.

Give me a look, give me a face,
That makes simplicity a grace;
Robes loosely flowing, hair as free,—
Such sweet neglect more taketh me
Than all the adulteries of art;
They strike mine eyes, but not mine heart.
           BEN JONSON.

II.

A SWEET disorder in the dress
Kindles in clothes a wantonness:
A lawn about the shoulders thrown
Into a fine distraction;
An erring lace, which here and there
Intrals the crimson stomacher;
A cuff neglectful, and thereby
Ribbons to flow confusedly;
A winning wave, deserving note,
In the tempestuous petticoat;
A careless shoestring, in whose tie
I see a wild civility,—
Do more bewitch me than when art
Is too precise in every part.
           ROBERT HERRICK.

THE EVE OF ST. AGNES.

I.

ST. AGNES' EVE—Ah, bitter chill it was!
The owl, for all his feathers, was a-cold;
The hare limped trembling through the
   frozen grass,
And silent was the flock in woolly fold:
Numb were the beadman's fingers while he
   told
His rosary, and while his frosted breath,
Like pious incense from a censer old,
Seemed taking flight for heaven without a
   death,
Past the sweet virgin's picture, while his
   prayer he saith.

II.

His prayer he saith, this patient, holy man;
Then takes his lamp, and riseth from his
   knees,
And back returneth, meagre, barefoot, wan,
Along the chapel aisle by slow degrees;
The sculptured dead, on each side seem to
   freeze,
Emprisoned in black, purgatorial rails;
Knights, ladies, praying in dumb orat'ries,
He passed by; and his weak spirit fails
To think how they may ache in icy hoods
   and mails.

III.

Northward he turneth through a little door,
And scarce three steps, ere music's golden
   tongue
Flattered to tears this aged man and poor;
But no—already had his death-bell rung;
The joys of all his life were said and sung;
His was harsh penance on St. Agnes' Eve;
Another way he went, and soon among
Rough ashes sat he for his soul's reprieve,
And all night kept awake, for sinners' sake
   to grieve.

IV.

That ancient beadsman heard the prelude
   soft;
And so it chanced, for many a door was
   wide,

COSTUME.

From hurry to and fro. Soon, up aloft,
The silver, snarling trumpets 'gan to chide;
The level chambers, ready with their pride,
Were glowing to receive a thousand guests;
The carved angels, ever eager-eyed,
Stared, where upon their heads the cornice
　　rests,
With hair blown back, and wings put
　　crosswise on their breasts.

V.

At length burst in the argent revelry,
With plume, tiara, and all rich array,
Numerous as shadows haunting fairily
The brain, new stuffed, in youth, with
　　triumphs gay
Of old romance. These let us wish away;
And turn, sole-thoughted, to one lady
　　there,
Whose heart had brooded, all that wintry
　　day,
On love, and winged St. Agnes' saintly
　　care,
As she had heard old dames full many
　　times declare.

VI.

They told her how, upon St. Agnes' Eve,
Young virgins might have visions of de-
　　light,
And soft adorings from their loves receive
Upon the honeyed middle of the night,
If ceremonies due they did aright;
As, supperless to bed they must retire,
And couch supine their beauties, lily white;
Nor look behind, nor sideways, but require
Of heaven with upward eyes for all that
　　they desire.

VII.

Full of this whim was thoughtful Madeline;
The music, yearning like a god in pain,
She scarcely heard; her maiden eyes divine,
Fixed on the floor, saw many a sweeping
　　train
Pass by—she heeded not at all; in vain
Came many a tiptoe, amorous cavalier,
And back retired; not cooled by high dis-
　　dain,

But she saw not; her heart was otherwhere;
She sighed for Agnes' dreams, the sweetest
　　of the year.

VIII.

She danced along with vague, regardless
　　eyes,
Anxious her lips, her breathing quick and
　　short;
The hallowed hour was near at hand; she
　　sighs
Amid the timbrels, and the thronged resort
Of whisperers in anger, or in sport;
Mid looks of love, defiance, hate, and scorn,
Hoodwinked with fairy fancy; all amort
Save to St. Agnes and her lambs unshorn,
And all the bliss to be before to-morrow
　　morn.

IX.

So, purposing each moment to retire,
She lingered still. Meantime across the
　　moors,
Had come young Porphyro, with heart on
　　fire
For Madeline. Beside the portal doors,
Buttressed from moonlight, stands he, and
　　implores
All saints to give him sight of Madeline;
But for one moment in the tedious hours,
That he might gaze and worship all un-
　　seen;
Perchance speak, kneel, touch, kiss—in
　　sooth such things have been.

X.

He ventures in; let no buzzed whisper tell;
All eyes be muffled, or a hundred swords
Will storm his heart, love's feverous citadel;
For him, those chambers held barbarian
　　hordes,
Hyena foemen, and hot-blooded lords,
Whose very dogs would execrations howl
Against his lineage; not one breast affords
Him any mercy, in that mansion foul,
Save one old beldame, weak in body and in
　　soul.

XI.

Ah, happy chance! the aged creature came,
Shuffling along with ivory-headed wand,
To where he stood, hid from the torch's
    flame,
Behind a broad hall-pillar, far beyond
The sound of merriment and chorus bland.
He startled her; but soon she knew his face
And grasped his fingers in her palsied hand.
Saying, "Mercy, Porphyro! hie thee from
  .   this place;
They are all here to-night, the whole blood-
    thirsty race!

XII.

"Get hence! get hence! there's dwarfish
    Hildebrand;
He had a fever late, and in the fit
He cursed thee and thine, both house and
    land;
Then there's that old Lord Maurice, not a
    whit
More tame for his gray hairs—Alas me! flit!
Flit like a ghost away!"—"Ah, gossip dear,
We're safe enough; here in this arm-chair
    sit,
And tell me how"—"Good saints, not here,
    not here;
Follow me, child, or else these stones will
    be thy bier."

XIII.

He followed through a lowly arched way,
Brushing the cobwebs with his lofty plume;
And as she muttered "Well-a—well-a-day!"
He found him in a little moonlight room,
Pale, latticed, chill, and silent as a tomb.
"Now tell me where is Madeline," said he,
"Oh, tell me, Angela, by the holy loom
Which none but secret sisterhood may see,
When they St. Agnes' wool are weaving
    piously."

XIV.

"St. Agnes! Ah! it is St. Agnes' Eve—
Yet men will murder upon holy days;
Thou must hold water in a witch's sieve,

And be liege-lord of all the elves and fays,
To venture so. It fills me with amaze
To see thee Porphyro!—St. Agnes' Eve!
God's help! my lady fair the conjurer plays
This very night; good angels her deceive!
But let me laugh awhile, I've mickle time
    to grieve"

XV.

Feebly she laugheth in the languid moon,
While Porphyro upon her face doth look,
Like puzzled urchin on an aged crone
Who keepeth closed a wondrous riddle-
    book,
As spectacled she sits in chimney nook.
But soon his eyes grew brilliant, when she
    told
His lady's purpose; and he scarce could
    brook
Tears, at the thought of those enchantments
    cold,
And Madeline asleep in lap of legends old.

XVI.

Sudden a thought came like a full-blown
    rose,
Flushing his brow, and in his pained heart
Made purple riot; then doth he propose
A stratagem, that makes the beldame start;
"A cruel man and impious thou art!
Sweet lady, let her pray and sleep and
    dream
Alone with her good angels, far apart
From wicked men like thee. Go, go! I
    deem
Thou canst not surely be the same that thou
    didst seem."

XVII.

"I will not harm her, by all saints I swear!"
Quoth Porphyro; "Oh may I ne'er find
    grace
When my weak voice shall whisper its last
    prayer,
If one of her soft ringlets I displace,
Or look with ruffian passion in her face;
Good Angela, believe me by these tears,

Or I will, even in a moment's space,
Awake, with horrid shout, my foemen's
ears,
And beard them, though they be more
fanged than wolves and bears."

XVIII.

"Ah! why wilt thou affright a feeble soul?
A poor, weak, palsy-stricken, church-yard
thing,
Whose passing-bell may ere the midnight
toll;
Whose prayers for thee, each morn and
evening,
Were never missed." Thus plaining doth
she bring
A gentler speech from burning Porphyro;
So woful, and of such deep sorrowing,
That Angela gives promise she will do
Whatever he shall wish, betide her weal or
woe.

XIX.

Which was, to lead him, in close secrecy,
Even to Madeline's chamber, and there hide
Him in a closet, of such privacy
That he might see her beauty unespied,
And win perhaps that night a peerless
bride;
While legioned fairies paced the coverlet,
And pale enchantment held her sleepy-
eyed.
Never on such a night have lovers met,
Since Merlin paid his demon all the mon-
strous debt.

XX.

"It shall be as thou wishest," said the dame;
"All cates and dainties shall be stored there
Quickly on this feast-night; by the tambour
frame
Her own lute thou wilt see; no time to
spare,
For I am slow and feeble, and scarce dare
On such a catering trust my dizzy head.
Wait here, my child, with patience kneel
in prayer
The while. Ah! thou must needs the lady
wed,

Or may I never leave my grave among the
dead."

XXI.

So saying she hobbled off with busy fear.
The lover's endless minutes slowly pass'd:
The dame return'd, and whisper'd in his ear
To follow her; with aged eyes aghast
From fright of dim espial. Safe at last,
Through many a dusky gallery, they gain
The maiden's chamber, silken, hush'd and
chaste;
Where Porphyro took covert, pleas'd amain.
His poor guide hurried back with agues in
her brain.

XXII.

Her faltering hand upon the balustrade,
Old Angela was feeling for the stair,
When Madeline, St. Agnes' charmed maid,
Rose, like a missioned spirit, unaware;
With silver taper's light, and pious care,
She turned, and down the aged gossip led
To a safe level matting. Now prepare,
Young Porphyro, for gazing on that bed!
She comes, she comes again, like ring-dove
frayed and fled.

XXIII.

Out went the taper as she hurried in;
Its little smoke, in pallid moonshine, died;
She closed the door, she panted, all akin
To spirits of the air, and visions wide;
No uttered syllable, or woe betide!
But to her heart, her heart was voluble,
Paining with eloquence her balmy side;
As though a tongueless nightingale should
swell
Her throat in vain, and die, heart-stifled in
her dell.

XXIV.

A casement high and triple-arched there
was,
All garlanded with carven imageries
Of fruits, and flowers, and bunches of knot-
grass,
And diamonded with pains of quaint device,
Innumerable of stains and splendid dyes,

As are the tiger-moth's deep-damasked
      wings;
And in the midst, 'mong thousand herald-
      ries,
And twilight saints, and dim emblazonings,
A shielded 'scutcheon blushed with blood
      of queens and kings.

XXV.

Full on this casement shone the wintry
      moon,
And threw warm gules on Madeline's fair
      breast,
As down she knelt for heaven's grace and
      boon;
Rose-bloom fell on her hands, together
      prest,
And on her silver cross soft amethyst,
And on her hair a glory, like a saint;
She seemed a splendid angel, newly drest,
Save wings, for heaven. Porphyro grew
      faint
She knelt, so pure a thing, so free from
      mortal taint.

XXVI.

Anon his heart revives; her vespers done,
Of all its wreathed pearls her hair she frees;
Unclasps her warmed jewels one by one;
Loosens her fragrant bodice; by degrees
Her rich attire creeps rustling to her knees;
Half-hidden, like a mermaid in sea-weed,
Pensive awhile she dreams awake, and sees,
In fancy, fair St. Agnes in her bed,
But dares not look behind, or all the charm
      is fled.

XXVII.

Soon, trembling in her soft and chilly nest,
In sort of wakeful swoon, perplexed she lay,
Until the poppied warmth of sleep oppressed
Her soothed limbs, and soul fatigued away;
Flown like a thought, until the morrow-day;
Blissfully havened both from joy and pain;
Clasped like a missal where swart Paynims
      pray;
Blinded alike from sunshine and from rain,
As though a rose should shut, and be a bud
      again.

XXVIII.

Stolen to this paradise, and so entranced,
Porphyro gazed upon her empty dress,
And listened to her breathing, if it chanced
To wake into a slumberous tenderness;
Which when he heard, that minute did he
      bless,
And breathed himself; then from the closet
      crept,
Noiseless as fear in a wide wilderness,
And over the hushed carpet, silent, stept,
And 'tween the curtains peeped, where,
      lo!—how fast she slept.

XXIX.

Then by the bed-side where the faded moon
Made a dim, silver twilight, soft he set
A table, and, half anguished, threw thereon
A cloth of woven crimson, gold, and jet:—
Oh for some drowsy Morphean amulet!
The boisterous, midnight, festive clarion,
The kettle-drum and far-heard clarionet;
Affray his ears, though but in dying tone:—
The hall-door shuts again, and all the noise
      is gone.

XXX.

And still she slept an azure-lidded sleep,
In blanched linen, smooth, and lavendered;
While he from forth the closet brought a
      heap
Of candied apple, quince, and plum, and
      gourd;
With jellies soother than the creamy curd,
And lucent syrups, tinct with cinnamon;
Manna and dates, in argosy transferred
From Fez; and spiced dainties, every one,
From silken Samarcand to cedared Leban-
      on.

XXXI.

These delicates he heaped with glowing
      hand
On golden dishes and in baskets bright
Of wreathed silver. Sumptuous they stand
In the retired quiet of the night,
Filling the chilly room with perfume
      light.—

"And now, my love, my seraph fair awake!
Thou art my heaven, and I thine eremite;
Open thine eyes, for meek St. Agnes' sake,
Or I shall drowse beside thee, so my soul
    doth ache."

XXXII.

Thus whispering, his warm, unnerved arm
Sank in her pillow. Shaded was her dream
By the dusk curtains;—'t was a midnight
    charm
Impossible to melt as iced stream:
The lustrous salvers in the moonlight
    gleam;
Broad golden fringe upon the carpet lies;
It seemed he never, never could redeem
From such a steadfast spell his lady's eyes;
So mused awhile, entoiled in woofed phan-
    tasies.

XXXIII.

Awakening up, he took her hollow lute,—
Tumultuous,—and, in chords that tenderest
    be,
He played an ancient ditty, long since mute,
In Provence called "La belle dame sans
    mercy;"
Close to her ear touching the melody;—
Wherewith disturbed, she uttered a soft
    moan;
He ceased—she panted quick—and sud-
    denly
Her blue eyes affrayed wide open shone;
Upon his knees he sank, pale as smooth-
    sculptured stone.

XXXIV.

Her eyes were open, but she still beheld,
Now wide awake, the vision of her sleep.
There was a painful change, that nigh ex-
    pelled
The blisses of her dream so pure and deep;
At which fair Madeline began to weep,
And moan forth witless words with many
    a sigh;
While still her gaze on Porphyro would
    keep,
Who knelt, with joined hands and piteous
    eye,

Fearing to move or speak, she looked so
    dreamingly.

XXXV.

"Ah, Porphyro!" said she, "but even now
Thy voice was at sweet tremble in mine
    ear,
Made tunable with every sweetest vow;
And those sad eyes were spiritual and clear;
How changed thou art! how pallid, chill,
    and drear!
Give me that voice again, my Porphyro,
Those looks immortal, those complainings
    dear!
Oh leave me not in this eternal woe,
For if thou diest, my love, I know not
    where to go."

XXXVI.

Beyond a mortal man impassioned far
At these voluptuous accents, he arose,
Ethereal, flushed, and like a throbbing star
Seen 'mid the sapphire heaven's deep re-
    pose;
Into her dream he melted, as the rose
Blendeth its odor with the violet,—
Solution sweet; meantime the frost-wind
    blows
Like love's alarum pattering the sharp sleet
Against the window-panes; St. Agnes'
    moon hath set.

XXXVII.

'T is dark; quick pattereth the flaw-blown
    sleet;
"This is no dream, my bride, my Made-
    line!"
'T is dark; the iced gusts still rave and beat:
"No dream, alas! alas! and woe is mine!
Porphyro will leave me here to fade and
    pine.—
Cruel! what traitor could thee hither bring?
I curse not, for my heart is lost in thine,
Though thou forsakest a deceived thing;—
A dove forlorn and lost, with sick, unprun-
    ed wing."

XXXVIII.

"My Madeline! sweet dreamer! lovely
    bride!
Say, may I be for aye thy vassal blest?
Thy beauty's shield, heart shaped and
    vermeil dyed?
Ah, silver shrine, here will I take my rest
After so many hours of toil and quest,
A famished pilgrim,—saved by miracle.
Though I have found, I will not rob thy nest
Saving of thy sweet self; if thou think'st
    well
To trust, fair Madeline, to no rude infidel.

XXXIX.

"Hark! 't is an elfin storm from fairy land,
Of haggard seeming, but a boon indeed:
Arise—arise! the morning is at hand;—
The bloated wassailers will never heed.
Let us away, my love, with happy speed;
There are no ears to hear, or eyes to see,—
Drowned all in Rhenish and the sleepy
    mead.
Awake! arise! my love, and fearless be,
For o'er the southern moors I have a
    home for thee."

XL.

She hurried at his words, beset with fears,
For there were sleeping dragons all around,
At glaring watch, perhaps with ready
    spears—
Down the wide stairs a darkling way they
    found,
In all the house was heard no human sound.
A chain-drooped lamp was flickering by
    each door;
The arras, rich with horseman, hawk, and
    hound,
Fluttered in the besieging wind's uproar;
And the long carpets rose along the gusty
    floor.

XLI.

They glide, like phantoms, into the wide
    hall!
Like phantoms to the iron porch they glide,
Where lay the porter, in uneasy sprawl,
With a huge empty flagon by his side;

The wakeful bloodhound rose, and shook
    his hide,
But his sagacious eye an inmate owns;
By one, and one, the bolts full easy slide:
The chains lie silent on the footworn
    stones:
The key turns, and the door upon its
    hinges groans.

XLII.

And they are gone! ay, ages long ago
These lovers fled away into the storm.
That night the baron dreamt of many a
    woe,
And all his warrior-guests, with shade and
    form
Of witch, and demon, and large coffin-
    worm,
Were long be-nightmared. Angela the old
Died palsy-twitched, with meagre face de-
    form;
The beadsman, after thousand aves told,
For aye, unsought-for slept among his
    ashes cold.

JOHN KEATS.

CAUGHT.

ON a day, (alack the day!)
Love, whose month was ever May,
Spied a blossom passing fair,
Playing in the wanton air:
Through the velvet leaves the wind
All unseen, 'gan passage find;
That the lover, sick to death,
Wish'd himself the heaven's breath.
Air, quoth he, thy cheeks may blow;
Air, would I might triumph so!
But, alas! my hand hath sworn
Ne'er to pluck thee from thy thorn.
Vow, alack, for youth unmeet;
Youth, so apt to pluck a sweet.
Do not call it sin in me,
That I am forsworn for thee
Thou, for whom even Jove would swear
Juno but an Ethiop were;
And deny himself for Jove,
Turning mortal for thy love.

—SHAKSPEARE.

CAUGHT.

THE MOTHER'S LAST SONG.

Sleep!—The ghostly winds are blowing!
No moon abroad—no star is glowing;
The river is deep, and the tide is flowing
To the land where you and I are going!
    We are going afar,
    Beyond moon or star,
  To the land where the sinless angels are!

I lost my heart to your heartless sire,
('T was melted away by his looks of fire)—
Forgot my God, and my father's ire,
All for the sake of a man's desire;
    But now we 'll go
    Where the waters flow,
And make us a bed where none shall
    know.

The world is cruel—the world is untrue;
Our foes are many, our friends are few;
No work, no bread, however we sue!
What is there left for me to do,
    But fly—fly
    From the cruel sky,
And hide in the deepest deeps—and die!
          Barry Cornwall.

THE SONG OF THE SHIRT.

With fingers weary and worn,
  With eyelids heavy and red,
A woman sat, in unwomanly rags,
  Plying her needle and thread—
    Stitch! stitch! stitch!
In poverty, hunger, and dirt;
  And still with a voice of dolorous pitch
She sang the "Song of the Shirt!"

"Work! work! work!
  While the cock is crowing aloof!
And work—work—work,
  Till the stars shine through the roof!
It 's oh! to be a slave
  Along with the barbarous Turk,
Where woman has never a soul to save,
  If this is Christian work!

"Work—work—work
  Till the brain begins to swim!
Work—work—work
  Till the eyes are heavy and dim!
Seam, and gusset, and band,
  Band, and gusset, and seam,
Till over the buttons I fall asleep,
  And sew them on in a dream!

"O men, with sisters dear!
  O men, with mothers and wives!
It is not linen you 're wearing out,
  But human creature's lives!
    Stitch—stitch—stitch,
  In poverty, hunger, and dirt—
Sewing at once, with a double thread,
  A shroud as well as a shirt!

"But why do I talk of death—
  That phantom of grisly bone?
I hardly fear his terrible shape,
  It seems so like my own—
  It seems so like my own
  Because of the fasts I keep;
O God! that bread should be so dear,
  And flesh and blood so cheap!

"Work—work—work!
  My labor never flags;
And what are its wages? A bed of straw
  A crust of bread—and rags,
That shattered roof—and this naked floor—
  A table—a broken chair—
And a wall so blank my shadow I thank
  For sometimes falling there!

"Work—work—work!
  From weary chime to chime!
Work—work—work—
  As prisoners work for crime!
Band, and gusset, and seam,
  Seam, and gusset, and band—
Till the heart is sick and the brain be-
    numbed,
  As well as the weary hand.

"Work—work—work
  In the dull December light!
And work—work—work,
  When the weather is warm and bright!—
While underneath the eaves

The brooding swallows cling,
As if to show me their sunny backs,
   And twit me with the Spring.

" Oh! but to breathe the breath
   Of the cowslip and primrose sweet—
With the sky above my head,
   And the grass beneath my feet!
For only one short hour
   To feel as I used to feel,
Before I knew the woes of want
   And the walk that costs a meal!

" Oh! but for one short hour—
   A respite however brief!
No blessed leisure for love or hope,
   But only time for grief!
A little weeping would ease my heart;
   But in their briny bed
My tears must stop, for every drop
   Hinders needle and thread!"

With fingers weary and worn,
   With eyelids heavy and red,
A woman sat, in unwomanly rags,
   Plying her needle and thread—
     Stitch! stitch! stitch!
   In poverty, hunger, and dirt;
And still, with a voice of dolorous pitch—
   Would that its tone could reach the rich!—
She sang this " Song of the Shirt!"

             THOMAS HOOD.

CONSTANCY.

ONE eve of beauty, when the sun,
   Was on the stream of Guadalquiver,
To gold converting one by one,
   The ripples of the mighty river,
Beside me on the bank was seated
   A Seville girl, with auburn hair
And eyes that might the world have
     cheated,—
   A wild bright, wicked, diamond pair!

She stooped and wrote upon the sand,
   Just as the loving sun was going,
With such a soft, small, shining hand,

I could have sworn 't was silver flowing.
Her words were three, and not one more,
   What could Diana's motto be?
The siren wrote upon the shore,—
   " Death, not inconstancy."

And then her two large languid eyes
   So turned on mine that, devil take me,
I set the air on fire with sighs,
   And was the fool she chose to make me!
Saint Francis would have been deceived
   With such an eye and such a hand;
But one week more, and I believed
   As much the woman as the sand.
            —ANONYMOUS.

EXCELSIOR.

THE shades of night were falling fast,
As through an Alpine village passed
A youth, who bore, 'mid snow and ice,
A banner with the strange device—
     Excelsior!

His brow was sad; his eye beneath
Flashed like a faulchion from its sheath;
And like a silver clarion rung
The accents of that unknown tongue—
     Excelsior!

In happy homes he saw the light
Of household fires gleam warm and bright,
Above, the spectral glaciers shone,
And from his lips escaped a groan—
     Excelsior!

" Try not the pass," the old man said:
" Dark lowers the tempest overhead;
The roaring torrent is deep and wide!"
And loud that clarion voice replied,
     Excelsior!

" Oh stay," the maiden said, " and rest
Thy weary head upon this breast!"
A tear stood in his bright blue eye,
But still he answered, with a sigh,
     Excelsior!

CONSTANCY.

"Beware the pine-tree's withered branch!
Beware the awful avalanche!"
This was the peasant's last good-night:
A voice replied, far up the height,
  Excelsior!

At break of day, as heavenward
The pious monks of Saint Bernard
Uttered the oft-repeated prayer,
A voice cried, through the startled air,
  Excelsior!

A traveller, by the faithful hound,
Half-buried in the snow was found,
Still grasping in his hand of ice
That banner with the strange device,
  Excelsior!

There in the twilight cold and gray,
Lifeless, but beautiful, he lay,
And from the sky, serene and far,
A voice fell, like a falling star—
  Excelsior!
  HENRY WADSWORTH LONGFELLOW.

THANATOPSIS.

To him who in the love of nature holds
Communion with her visible forms, she
 speaks
A various language; for his gayer hours
She has a voice of gladness, and a smile
And eloquence of beauty; and she glides
Into his darker musings with a mild
And healing sympathy, that steals away
Their sharpness ere he is aware. When
 thoughts
Of the last bitter hour come like a blight
Over thy spirit, and sad images
Of the stern agony, and shroud, and pall,
And breathless darkness, and the narrow
 house,
Make thee to shudder, and grow sick at
 heart—
Go forth, under the open sky, and list
To nature's teachings, while from all
 around—
Earth and her waters, and the depths
 of air—

Comes a still voice: Yet a few days, and thee
The all-beholding sun shall see no more
In all his course; nor yet in the cold
 ground,
Where thy pale form was laid with many
 tears,
Nor in the embrace of ocean shall exist
Thy image. Earth, that nourished thee,
 shall claim
Thy growth to be resolved to earth again;
And, lost each human trace, surrendering
 up
Thine individual being, shalt thou go
To mix for ever with the elements—
To be a brother to the insensible rock,
And to the sluggish clod which the rude
 swain
Turns with his snare, and treads upon. The
 oak
Shall send his roots abroad, and pierce thy
 mould.

Yet not to thine eternal resting-place
Shalt thou retire alone, nor couldst thou
 wish
Couch more magnificent. Thou shalt lie
 down
With patriarchs of the infant world—with
 kings,
The powerful of the earth—the wise, the
 good—
Fair forms, and hoary seers of ages past
All in one mighty sepulchre. The hills
Rock-ribbed and ancient as the sun,—the
 vales
Stretching in pensive quietness between—
The venerable woods—rivers that move
In majesty, and the complaining brooks
That make the meadows green; and, poured
 round all,
Old ocean's gray and melancholy waste,—
Are but the solemn decorations all
Of the great tomb of man. The golden sun,
The planets, all the infinite host of heaven,
Are shining on the sad abodes of death,
Through the still lapse of ages. All that
 tread
The globe are but a handful to the tribes
That slumber in its bosom.—Take the
 wings

Of morning; traverse Barca's desert sands,
Or lose thyself in the continuous woods
Where rolls the Oregon, and hears no
sound
Save his own dashings—yet— the dead are
there;
And millions in those solitudes, since first
The flight of years began, have laid them
down
In their last sleep—the dead reign there
alone.
So shalt thou rest; and what if thou with-
draw
In silence from the living, and no friend
Take note of thy departure?   All that
breathe
Will share thy destiny. The gay will laugh
When thou art gone, the solemn brood of
care
Plod on, and each one as before will chase
His favorite phantom; yet all these shall
leave
Their mirth and their employments, and
shall come
And make their bed with thee. As the
long train
Of ages glide away, the sons of men,
The youth in life's green spring, and he
who goes
In the full strength of years—matron, and
maid,
And the sweet babe, and the gray-headed
man,—
Shall one by one be gathered to thy side
By those, who in their turn shall follow
them.

So live, that when thy summons comes
to join
The innumerable caravan which moves
To that mysterious realm where each shall
take
His chamber in the silent halls of death,
Thou go not like the quarry-slave at night,
Scourged to his dungeon; but, sustained
and soothed
By an unfaltering trust, approach thy
grave

Like one who wraps the drapery of his
couch
About him, and lies down to pleasant
dreams.
                    WILLIAM CULLEN BRYANT.

THE DIVERTING HISTORY OF
JOHN GILPIN,

SHOWING HOW HE WENT FARTHER THAN
HE INTENDED, AND CAME SAFE
HOME AGAIN.

JOHN GILPIN was a citizen
    Of credit and renown;
A trainband captain eke was he,
    Of famous London town.

John Gilpin's spouse said to her dear—
    "Though wedded we have been
These twice ten tedious years, yet we
    No holiday have seen.

"To-morrow is our wedding day,
    And we will then repair
Unto the Bell at Edmonton
    All in a chaise and pair.

"My sister, and my sister's child,
    Myself and children three,
Will fill the chaise; so you must ride
    On horseback after we."

He soon replied, "I do admire
    Of womankind but one,
And you are she, my dearest dear;
    Therefore it shall be done.

"I am a linendraper bold,
    As all the world doth know;
And my good friend, the calender,
    Will lend his horse to go."

Quoth Mrs. Gilpin, "That's well said;
    And, for that wine is dear,
We will be furnished with our own,
    Which is both bright and clear."

John Gilpin kissed his loving wife;
  O'erjoyed was he to find
That, though on pleasure she was bent,
  She had a frugal mind.

The morning came, the chaise was brought,
  But yet was not allowed
To drive up to the door, lest all
  Should say that she was proud.

So three doors off the chaise was stayed
  Where they did all get in—
Six precious souls, and all agog
  To dash through thick and thin.

Smack went the whip, round went the
    wheels—
Were never folks so glad;
The stones did rattle underneath,
  As if Cheapside were mad.

John Gilpin at his horse's side
  Seized fast the flowing mane,
And up he got, in haste to ride—
  But soon came down again:

For saddletree scarce reached had he,
  His journey to begin,
When, turning round his head, he saw
  Three customers come in.

So down he came: for loss of time,
  Although it grieved him sore,
Yet loss of pence, full well he knew,
  Would trouble him much more.

'T was long before the customers
  Were suited to their mind;
When Betty, screaming, came down stairs—
  "The wine is left behind!"

"Good lack!" quoth he—"yet bring it me,
  My leathern belt likewise,
In which I bear my trusty sword
  When I do exercise."

Now Mistress Gilpin (careful soul!)
  Had two stone bottles found,
To hold the liquor that she loved,
  And keep it safe and sound.

Each bottle had a curling ear,
  Through which the belt he drew,
And hung a bottle on each side,
  To make his balance true.

Then over all, that he might be
  Equipped from top to toe.
His long red cloak, well brushed and neat,
  He manfully did throw.

Now see him mounted once again
  Upon his nimble steed,
Full slowly pacing o'er the stones,
  With caution and good heed.

But finding soon a smoother road
  Beneath his well shod feet,
The snorting beast began to trot,
  Which galled him in his seat.

So, "Fair and softly," John he cried,
  But John he cried in vain;
That trot became a gallop soon.
  In spite of curb and rein.

So stooping down, as needs he must
  Who cannot sit upright,
He grasped the mane with both his hands,
  And eke with all his might.

His horse, who never in that sort
  Had handled been before,
What thing upon his back had got
  Did wonder more and more.

Away went Gilpin, neck or nought;
  Away went hat and wig;
He little dreamt, when he set out,
  Of running such a rig.

The wind did blow—the cloak did fly,
  Like streamer long and gay;
Till, loop and button failing both,
  At last it flew away.

Then might all people well discern
  The bottles he had slung—
A bottle swinging at each side,
  As hath been said or sung.

The dogs did bark, the children screamed,
  Up flew the windows all;
And every soul cried out, " Well done!"
  As loud as he could bawl.

Away went Gilpin—who but he?
  His fame soon spead around—
" He carries weight! he rides a race!
  'T is for a thousand pound!"

And still as fast as he drew near,
  ' 'T was wonderful to view
How in a trice the turnpike men
  Their gates wide open threw.

And now, as he went bowing down
  His reeking head full low,
The bottles twain behind his back,
  Were shattered at a blow.

Down ran the wine into the road,
  Most piteous to be seen,
Which made his horse's flanks to smoke
  As they had basted been.

But still he seemed to carry weight,
  With leathern girdle braced;
For all might see the bottle necks
  Still dangling at his waist.

Thus all through merry Islington
  These gambols did he play,
Until he came unto the Wash
  Of Edmonton so gay:

And there he threw the wash about
  On both sides of the way,
Just like unto a trundling mop,
  Or a wild goose at play.

At Edmonton his loving wife
  From the balcony spied
Her tender husband, wondering much
  To see how he did ride.

" Stop, stop, John Gilpin! here's the house
  They all at once did cry;
" The dinner waits, and we are tired : "
  Said Gilpin—" So am I!"

But yet his horse was not a whit
  Inclined to tarry there;
For why?—his owner had a house
  Full ten miles off, at Ware.

So like an arrow swift he flew,
  Shot by an archer strong;
So did he fly—which brings me to
  The middle of my song.

Away went Gilpin out of breath,
  And sore against his will,
Till at his friend the calender's
  His horse at last stood still.

The calender, amazed to see
  His neighbor in such trim,
Laid down his pipe, flew to the gate,
  · And thus accosted him:

"What news? what news? your tidings tell;
  Tell me you must and shall—
Say why bareheaded you are come,
  Or why you come at all?"

Now Gilpin had a pleasant wit,
  And loved a timely joke;
And thus unto the calender
  In merry guise he spoke:

" I came because your horse would come;
  And, if I well forbode,
My hat and wig will soon be here,
  They are upon the road."

The calender, right glad to find
  His friend in merry pin,
Returned him not a single word,
  But to the house went in;

Whence straight he came with hat and wig.
  A wig that flowed behind,
A hat not much the worse for wear—
  Each comely in its kind.

He held them up, and in his turn
  Thus showed his ready wit—
" My head is twice as big as yours,
  They therefore needs must fit.

" But let me scrape the dirt away
  That hangs upon your face;
And stop and eat, for well you may
  Be in a hungry case."

Said John, " It is my wedding day,
  And all the world would stare
If wife should dine at Edmonton,
  And I should dine at Ware."

So turning to his horse, he said
  " I am in haste to dine;
'T was for your pleasure you came here—
  You shall go back for mine."

Ah, luckless speech, and bootless boast,
  For which he paid full dear!
For, while he spake, a braying ass
  Did sing most loud and clear;

Whereat his horse did snort, as he
  Had heard a lion roar,
And galloped off with all his might,
  As he had done before.

Away went Gilpin, and away
  Went Gilpin's hat and wig:
He lost them sooner than at first,
  For why?—they were too big.

Now Mistress Gilpin, when she saw
  Her husband posting down
Into the country far away,
  She pulled out half a crown;

And thus unto the youth she said,
  That drove them to the Bell,
" This shall be yours when you bring back
  My husband safe and well."

The youth did ride, and soon did meet
  John coming back amain—
Whom in a trice he tried to stop,
  By catching at his rein;

But not performing what he meant,
  And gladly would have done,
The frighted steed he frighted more,
  And made him faster run.

Away went Gilpin, and away
  Went post-boy at his heels,
The post-boy's horse right glad to miss
  The lumbering of the wheels.

Six gentlemen upon the road,
  Thus seeing Gilpin fly,
With post-boy scampering in the rear,
  They raised the hue and cry:

" Stop thief! stop thief!—a highwayman!"
  Not one of them was mute;
And all and each that passed that way
  Did join in the pursuit.

And now the turnpike gates again
  Flew open in short space;
The toll-men thinking as before,
  That Gilpin rode a race.

And so he did, and won it too,
  For he got first to town;
Nor stopped till where he had got up
  He did again get down.

Now let us sing, long live the king!
  And Gilpin, long live he;
And when he next doth ride abroad,
  May I be there to see!

                    WILLIAM COWPER.

THE MOURNER.

Yes! there are real mourners,—I have seen
A fair sad girl, mild, suffering, and serene;
Attention (through the day) her duties
    claimed,
And to be useful as resigned she aimed,
Neatly she drest, nor vainly seemed t' expect
Pity for grief or pardon for neglect;
But when her wearied parents sunk to sleep,
She sought her place to meditate and weep;
Then to her mind was all the past displayed,
That faithful memory brings to sorrow's aid:
For then she thought on one regretted
    youth,
Her tender trust, and his unquestioned
    truth;

In every place she wandered where they 'd
been,
And sadly-sacred held the parting scene,
Where last for sea he took his leave; that
place
With double interest would she nightly
trace!
　Happy he sailed, and great the care she
took
That he should softly sleep and smartly look;
White was his better linen, and his cheek
Was made more trim than any on the deck;
And every comfort men at sea can know
Was hers to buy, to make, and to bestow:
For he to Greenland sailed, and much she
told
How he should guard against the climate's
cold
Yet saw not danger; dangers he'd withstood,
Nor could she trace the fever in his blood.
　His messmates smiled at flushings on
his cheek,
And he too smiled, but seldom would he
speak,
For now he found the danger, felt the pain,
With grievous symptoms he could not
explain.
He called his friend, and prefaced with a
sigh
A lover's message,—"Thomas, I must die;
Would I could see my Sally, and could rest
My throbbing temples on her faithful breast,
And gazing go!—if not, this trifle take,
And say, till death I wore it for her sake;
Yes! I must die—blow on, sweet breeze,
blow on!
Give me one look before my life be gone!
O, give me that, and let me not despair!
One last fond look!—and now repeat the
prayer."
　He had his wish, had more: I will not
paint
The lovers' meeting; she beheld him faint,—
With tender fears, she took a nearer view,
Her terrors doubling as her hopes with-
drew;
He tried to smile, and half succeeding said,
"Yes! I must die"—and hope forever fled.
　Still, long she nursed him; tender
thoughts meantime

Were interchanged, and hopes and views
sublime.
To her he came to die, and every day
She took some portion of the dread away;
With him she prayed, to him his Bible read,
Soothed the faint heart and held the aching
head;
She came with smiles the hour of pain to
cheer,
Apart she sighed; alone, she shed the tear;
Then, as if breaking from a cloud, she gave
Fresh light, and gilt the prospect of the
grave.
　One day he lighter seemed, and they
forgot
The care, the dread, the anguish of their lot.
A sudden brightness in his look appeared,
A sudden vigor in his voice was heard;—
She had been reading in the Book of Prayer,
And led him forth, and placed him in his
chair.
Lively he seemed, and spake of all he knew;
The friendly many, and the favorite few;
. . . . . but then his hand was prest,
And fondly whispered, "Thou must go to
rest."
"I go," he said; but as he spoke, she found
His hand more cold, and fluttering was the
sound;
Then gazed affrighted; but she caught a last
A dying look of love, and all was past!
She placed a decent stone his grave above,
Neatly engraved,—an offering of her love;
For that she wrought, for that forsook her
bed,
Awake alike to duty and the dead;
She would have grieved had friends pre-
sumed to spare
The least assistance,—'t was her proper
care.
Here will she come, and on the grave will
sit,
Folding her arms, in long abstracted fit;
But if observer pass, will take her round,
And careless seem, for she would not be
found;
Then go again, and thus her hours employ,
While visions please her, and while woes
destroy.

GEORGE CRABBE.

THE MOURNER.

THE BELLS.

I.

HEAR the sledges with the bells—
Silver bells—
What a world of merriment their melody
foretells!
How they tinkle, tinkle, tinkle,
In the icy air of night!
While the stars that oversprinkle
All the heavens, seem to twinkle
With a crystalline delight—
Keeping time, time, time,
In a sort of Runic rhyme,
To the tintinnabulation that so musically
wells
From the bells, bells, bells, bells,
Bells, bells, bells—
From the jingling and the tinkling of the
bells.

II.

Hear the mellow wedding bells—
Golden bells!
What a world of happiness their harmony
foretells!
Through the balmy air of night
How they ring out their delight!
From the molten-golden notes,
And all in tune,
What a liquid ditty floats
To the turtle-dove that listens, while she
gloats
On the moon!
Oh, from out the sounding cells,
What a gush of euphony voluminously
wells!
How it swells!
How it dwells
On the Future! how it tells
Of the rapture that impels
To the swinging and the ringing
Of the bells, bells, bells,
Of the bells, bells, bells, bells,
Bells, bells, bells—
To the rhyming and the chiming of the
bells

III.

Hear the loud alarum bells—
Brazen bells!
What a tale of terror, now, their turbulency
tells!
In the startled ear of night
How they scream out their affright
Too much horrified to speak,
They can only shriek, shriek,
Out of tune,
In the clamorous appealing to the mercy
of the fire,
In a mad expostulation with the deaf and
frantic fire
Leaping higher, higher, higher,
With a desperate desire,
And a resolute endeavor,
Now—now to sit or never,
By the side of the pale-faced moon.
Oh, the bells, bells, bells,
What a tale their terror tells
Of despair!
How they clang, and clash, and roar!
What a horror they outpour
On the bosom of the palpitating air!
Yet the ear it fully knows,
By the twanging
And the clanging,
How the danger ebbs and flows;
Yet the ear distinctly tells,
In the jangling,
And the wrangling,
How the danger sinks and sw ls,
By the sinking or the swelling in the nger
of the bells—
Of the bells—
Of the bells, bells, bells, bells,
Bells, bells, bells—
In the clamor and the clangor of the bells!

IV.

Hear the tolling of the bells—
Iron bells!
What a world of solemn thought their
monody compels!
In the silence of the night,
How we shiver with affright
At the melancholy menace of their tone!

For every sound that floats
From the rust within their throats
     Is a groan.
And the people—ah, the people—
They that dwell up in the steeple,
     All alone,
And who tolling, tolling, tolling,
  In that muffled monotone,
Feel a glory in so rolling
  On the human heart a stone—
They are neither man nor woman—
They are neither brute nor human—
     They are ghouls:
And their king it is who tolls;
And he rolls, rolls, rolls,
     Rolls,
  A pæan from the bells!
And his merry bosom swells
  With the pæan of the bells!
And he dances and he yells;
Keeping time, time, time,
In a sort of Runic rhyme,
  To the pæan of the bells—
     Of the bells:
Keeping time, time, time,
In a sort of Runic rhyme,
  To the throbbing of the bells—
Of the bells, bells, bells—
  To the sobbing of the bells;
Keeping time, time, time,
  As he knells, knells, knells,
In a happy Runic rhyme,
  To the rolling of the bells—
Of the bells, bells, bells—
  To the tolling of the bells,
Of the bells, bells, bells, bells—
     Bells, bells, bells—
To the moaning and the groaning of the
     bells.
          EDGAR ALLAN POE.

THOSE EVENING BELLS.

THOSE evening bells! those evening bells!
How many a tale their music tells,
Of youth, and home, and that sweet time
When last I heard their soothing chime!

Those joyous hours are passed away;
And many a heart that then was gay,
Within the tomb now darkly dwells,
And hears no more those evening bells.

And so 't will be when I am gone—
That tuneful peal will still ring on;
While other bards shall walk these dells,
And sing your praise; sweet evening bells.
          THOMAS MOORE.

THE LADY AT SEA.

CABLES entangling her;
Ship-spars for mangling her;
Ropes sure of strangling her;
Blocks over-dangling her;
Tiller to batter her;
Topmast to shatter her;
Tobacco to spatter her;
Boreas blustering;
Boatswain quite flustering;
Thunder-clouds mustering,
To blast her with sulphur—
If the deep do n't ingulph her;
Sometimes fear 's scrutiny
Pries out a mutiny,
Sniffs conflagration,
Or hints at starvation;
All the sea dangers,
Buccaneers, rangers,
Pirates, and Sallee-men,
Algerine galley-men,
Tornadoes and typhons,
And horrible syphons,
And submarine travels
Thro' roaring sea-navels;
Everything wrong enough—
Long-boat not long enough;
Vessel not strong enough;
Pitch marring frippery;
The deck very slippery;
And the cabin—built sloping;
The captain a-toping;
And the mate a blasphemer,
That names his Redeemer—
With inward uneasiness;

The cook known by greasiness·
The victuals beslubbered;
Her bed—in a cupboard;
Things of strange christening,
Snatched in her listening;
Blue lights and red lights,
And mention of dead lights;
And shrouds made a theme of—
Things horrid to dream of;
And buoys in the water;
To fear all exhort her.
Her friend no Leander—
Herself no sea gander:
And ne'er a cork jacket
On board of the packet;
The breeze still a-stiffening;
The trumpet quite deafening;
Thoughts of repentance,
And doomsday, and sentence;
Every thing sinister—
Not a church minister;
Pilot a blunderer;
Coral reefs under her,
Ready to sunder her:
Trunks tipsy-topsy;
The ship in a dropsy;
Waves oversurging her;
Sirens a-dirging her;
Sharks all expecting her;
Sword-fish dissecting her;
Crabs with their hand-vices
Punishing land vices;
Sea-dogs and unicorns,
Things with no puny horns;
Mermen carnivorous—
" Good Lord deliver us!"

THOMAS HOOD.

AULD ROBIN GRAY.

WHEN the sheep are in the fauld, and the
    kye at hame,
And a' the warld to sleep are gane;
The waes o' my heart fa' in showers frae
    my ee,
When my gudeman lies sound by me.

Young Jamie loo'd me weel; and socht me
    for his bride;

But, saving a croun, he had naething else
    beside.
To mak that croun a pund, young Jamie
    gaed to sea;
And the croun and the pund were baith for
    me!

He hadna been awa a week but only twa,
When my mother she fell sick, and the
    cow was stown awa;
My father brak his arm, and young Jamie
    at the sea—
And auld Robin Gray cam' a-courtin' me.

My father cou'dna work, and my mother
    cou'dna spin;
I toiled day and nicht, but their bread
    I cou'dna win;
Auld Rob maintained them baith, and,
    wi' tears in his ee,
Said, "Jenny, for their sakes, oh marry
    me!"

My heart it said nay, for I looked for Jamie
    back;
But the wind it blew high, and the ship it
    was a wrack;
The ship it was a wrack! Why didna Jamie
    dee?
Or, why do I live to say, Wae's me!

My father argued sair—my mother didna
    speak,
But she lookit in my face till my heart was
    like to break;
Sae they gied him my hand; though my
    heart was in the sea;
And auld Robin Gray was gudeman to me.

I hadna been a wife, a week but only four,
When, sitting sae mournfully at the door,
I saw my Jamie's wraith, for I cou'dna
    think it he,
Till he said, "I'm come back for to marry
    thee!"

Oh sair, sair did we greet, and muckle did
    we say;

We took but ae kiss, and we tore ourselves
    away;
I wish I were dead, but I 'm no like to dee;
And why do I live to say, Wae 's me?

I gang like a ghaist, and I carena to spin;
I daurna think on Jamie, for that wad be a
    sin;
But I 'll do my best a gude wife to be,
For auld Robin Gray is kind unto me.

LADY ANNE BARNARD.

·   ——

CHASTELARD TO MARY STUART.

DEAR heart, I bless you for this parting
    grace,
  That is as sunshine on a winter day;
Now that last looks may be upon your face,
  There nothing is can wound me on my way
Filling my prison with a light divine,
  My queen, you come as does a saintly
    moon,
And I forget the dark clouds while you shine
  And take no heed of that which will be
    soon.
Was ever fate like mine? so dark and sweet?
God's feast before me, and I may not eat.

God's feast, for I have won your heart at
    last,
  And may not tarry for a lover's kiss;
But rich reward for future pain and past
  Is this one hour—this present hour of
    bliss.
What though another night shall find me
    dead,
  With no more sense of love and summer
    morn:
I lived to put a crown upon my head
  That shall be with me in the time unborn;
Nor may I be deceived with dying breath—
Speech is prophetic on the day of death.

Trust me, my perfect love, this midnight
    walk
  Is but a fretful prologue to the play—
Anxietude and doubt and troubled talk,
  Then writing shows the scene for Heaven
    Day.

How tell you all in such a breathless time?
  When Death is standing with his door
    ajar,
Counting the minutes in a dreadful rhyme,
  Till he may take his whetted scythe,
    and mar
The glorious garden where my pleasures
    grew
To music and new hope because of you.

It is a fearful fall to truest knights—
  This headlong tumble to a mystic goal,
This slipping from God's sky and all its
    lights,
  To dirt and darkness in a narrow hole;
But unto me an angel came to show
  That we imagine all the bitter part—
One crack of thunder and one seething
    glow
  Of lightning, and a little timid start,
And there an end; the storm becomes a
    charm,
With promise of new life without alarm.

I do remember in Love's land of France,
  Whither best thoughts do truant-like run
    back,
Our life was zoned with light and fair ro-
    mance,
  And dance and glamour followed in the
    track—
Nay, these are not poor flow'rs I pluck so
    late;
  They have the scent of early love, and
    tho'
Some poison-buds come too, they are of
    Fate,
  And honey were not sweet if 't were not
    so;
All is for love, and deadly nightshade grows
As much by Heaven's will as does the rose.

When that the gentle Hero held the light,
  Leander, knowing then her truth to him,
Sank under sea in his extreme delight,
  And in Life's river could no longer swim:
Now that you hold this loving light to me,
  Death's river, where the clouds hang in
    the night,
Shall be as glorious as Leander's sea,

CHASTELARD TO MARY STUART.

And the mysterious ferry shall be bright;
Your tears are bitter-sweet, e'en I could
weep
For joy of this " Good night, and pleasant
sleep."

Stay your tears, my sweet, and no more
speech
Shall come from me of Death; if my
heart's kiss
Can cure your agony, I do beseech
Your lips a little, that I may not miss
The melody locked up with your dear voice.
This pure and precious time can no pain
give,
But only gentle faith, and I rejoice
In knowledge of love strong enough to
live:
Your hand is heaven, my love; I feel your
kiss:
Your eyes speak peace, and now the rest is
bliss.   GUY ROSLYN.

THE PIED PIPER OF HAMELIN.

I.

HAMELIN Town 's in Brunswick,
By famous Hanover city;
    The river Weser, deep and wide,
    Washes its wall on the southern side;
    A pleasanter spot you never spied;
But when begins my ditty,
    Almost five hundred years ago,
    To see the townsfolk suffer so
From vermin, was a pity.

II.

    Rats!
They fought the dogs, and killed the cats,
And bit the babies in the cradles,
And ate the cheeses out of the vats,
    And licked the soup from the cook's own
        ladles,
Split open the kegs of salted sprats,
Made nests inside men's Sunday hats,
And even spoiled the women's chats,

By drowning their speaking
    With shrieking and squeaking
In fifty different sharps and flats.

III.

At last the people in a body
    To the Town Hall came flocking:
" 'T is clear," cried they, "our Mayor 's a
        noddy;
    And as for our Corporation—shocking
To think we buy gowns lined with ermine
For dolts that can't or won't determine
What 's best to rid us of our vermin!
You hope, because you 're old and obese,
To find in the furry civic robe ease?
Rouse up, sirs! Give your brains a racking
To find the remedy we 're lacking,
Or, sure as fate, we 'll send you packing!"
At this the Mayor and Corporation
Quaked with a mighty consternation.

IV.

An hour they sate in counsel—
    At length the Mayor broke silence:
' For a guilder I 'd my ermine gown sell;
    I wish I were a mile hence!
It 's easy to bid one rack one's brain—
I 'm sure my poor head aches again,
I 've scratched it so, and all in vain.
Oh for a trap, a trap, a trap!"
Just as he said this, what should hap
At the chamber door but a gentle tap?
' Bless us," cried the Mayor, "what 's that?"
(With the Corporation as he sat,
Looking little though wondrous fat;
Nor brighter was his eye, nor moister
Than a too-long-opened oyster,
Save when at noon his paunch grew muti-
        nous
For a plate of turtle, green and glutinous)
" Only a scraping of shoes on the mat?
Anything like the sound of a rat
Makes my heart go pit-a-pat!"

V.

" Come in!" the Mayor cried, looking
        bigger;
And in did come the strangest figure:
His queer long coat from heel to head

Was half of yellow and half of red;
And he himself was tall and thin;
With sharp blue eyes each like a pin;
And light loose hair, yet swarthy skin;
No tuft on cheek nor beard on chin
But lips where smiles went out and in—
There was no guessing his kith and kin!
And nobody could enough admire
The tall man and his quaint attire.
Quoth one: "It's as my great-grandsire,
Starting up at the trump of doom's tone,
Had walked this way from his painted
    tombstone!"

VI.

He advanced to the council table:
And, "Please your honors," said he, I'm
    able,
By means of a secret charm, to draw
All living creatures beneath the sun,
That creep, or swim, or fly, or run,
After me so as you never saw!
And I chiefly use my charm
On creatures that do people harm—
The mole, and toad, and newt, and viper—
And people call me the Pied Piper."
(And here they noticed around his neck
A scarf of red and yellow stripe,
To match with his coat of the self same
    check;
And at the scarf's end hung a pipe;
And his fingers, they noticed, were ever
    straying
As if impatient to be playing
Upon this pipe, as low it dangled
Over his vesture so old-fangled.)
    Yet," said he, "poor piper as I am,
In Tartary I freed the Cham,
Last June, from his huge swarm of gnats;
I eased in Asia the Nizam
Of a monstrous brood of vampire-bats;
And, as for what your brain bewilders—
If I can rid your town of rats,
Will you give me a thousand guilders?"
"One? fifty thousand!"—was the exclama-
    tion
Of the astonished Mayor and Corporation.

VII.

Into the street the piper stept,
    Smiling first a little smile,
As if he knew what magic slept
    In his quiet pipe the while;
Then, like a musical adept,
To blow the pipe his lips he wrinkled,
And green and blue his sharp eyes twinkled
Like a candle flame where salt is sprinkled;
And ere three shrill notes the pipe uttered,
You heard as if an army muttered;
And the muttering grew to a grumbling;
And the grumbling grew to a mighty rum-
    bling;
And out of the houses the rats came tum-
    bling.
Great rats, small rats, lean rats, brawny rats,
Brown rats, black rats, grey rats, tawny rats,
Grave old plodders, gay young friskers,
    Fathers, mothers, uncles, cousins,
Cocking tails and pricking whiskers;
    Families by tens and dozens,
Brothers, sisters, husbands, wives—
Followed the Piper for their lives.
From street to street he piped advancing, ·
And step for step they followed dancing,
Until they came to the river Weser
Wherein all plunged and perished
—Save one who, stout as Julius Cæsar,
Swam across and lived to carry
(As he the manuscript he cherished)
To Rat-land home his commentary,
Which was: "At the first shrill notes of
    the pipe,
I heard a sound as of scraping tripe,
And putting apples, wondrous ripe,
Into a cider-press's gripe—
And a moving away of pickle-tub-boards,
And a leaving ajar of conserve-cupboards,
And a drawing the corks of train-oil-flasks,
And a breaking the hoops of butter-casks;
And it seemed as if a voice
(Sweeter far than by harp or by psaltery
Is breathed) called out, O rats, rejoice!
The world is grown to one vast drysaltery!
So munch on, crunch on, take your
    nuncheon,
Breakfast, supper, dinner, luncheon!
And just as a bulky sugar-puncheon,

All ready staved, like a great sun shone
Glorious, scarce an inch before me,
Just as methought it said, Come, bore me!
—I found the Weser rolling o'er me."

VIII.

You should have heard the Hamelin people
Ringing the bells till they rocked the
    steeple;
"Go," cried the Mayor, "and get long poles!
Poke out the nests and block up the holes!
Consult with carpenters and builders,
And leave in our town not even a trace
Of the rats!"—when suddenly, up the face
Of the Piper perked in the market-place,
With a, "First, if you please, my thousand
    guilders!"

IX.

A thousand guilders! The Mayor looked
    blue;
So did the Corporation too.
For council dinners made rare havock
With Claret, Moselle, Vin-de-Grave, Hock:
And half the money would replenish
Their cellar's biggest butt with Rhenish.
To pay this sum to a wandering fellow
With a gypsy coat of red and yellow!
"Beside," quoth the Mayor, with a knowing
    wink,
"Our business was done at the river's brink;
We saw with our eyes the vermin sink.
And what's dead can't come to life, I think,
So, friend, we're not the folks to shrink
From the duty of giving you something
    for drink,
And a matter of money to put in your poke;
But, as for the guilders, what we spoke
Of them, as you very well know, was in
    joke
Beside, our losses have made us thrifty;
A thousand guilders! Come, take fifty!"

X.

The piper's face fell, and he cried,
"No trifling! I can't wait! beside,
I've promised to visit by dinner time
Bagdat, and accept the prime

Of the head cook's pottage, all he's rich in,
For having left, in the Caliph's kitchen,
Of a nest of scorpion's no survivor—
With him I proved no bargain-driver;
With you, don't think I'll bate a stiver!
And folks who put me in a passion
May find me pipe to another fashion."

XI.

"How?" cried the Mayor, "d'ye think I'll
    brook
Being worse-treated than a cook?
Insulted by a lazy ribald
With idle pipe and vesture piebald?
You threaten us, fellow? Do your worst,
Blow your pipe there till you burst!"

XII.

Once more he stept into the street;
    And to his lips again
Laid his long pipe of smooth straight cane;
    And ere he blew three notes (such sweet
Soft notes as yet musician's cunning
    Never gave the enraptured air)
There was a rustling that seemed like a
    bustling
Of merry crowds justling at pitching and
    hustling;
Small feet were pattering, wooden shoes
    clattering,
Little hands clapping, and little tongues
    chattering;
And, like fowls in a farm-yard when barley
    is scattering,
Out came the children running:
All the little boys and girls,
With rosy cheeks and flaxen curls,
And sparkling eyes and teeth like pearls,
Tripping and skipping, ran merrily after
The wonderful music with shouting and
    laughter.

XIII.

The Mayor was dumb, and the Council
    stood
As if they were changed into blocks of
    wood,
Unable to move a step or cry

To the children merrily skipping by—
And could only follow with the eye
That joyous crowd at the Piper's back.
But how the Mayor was on the rack,
And the wretched Council's bosoms beat,
As the Piper turned from the High Street
To where the Weser rolled its waters
Right in the way of their sons and daughters!
However, he turned from South to West,
And to Koppelberg Hill his steps addressed,
And after him the children pressed;
Great was the joy in every breast.
" He never can cross that mighty top!
He 's forced to let the piping drop,
And we shall see our children stop!"
When, lo, as they reached the mountain's
side,
A wondrous portal opened wide,
As if a cavern was suddenly hollowed;
And the Piper advanced and the children
followed;
And when all were in to the very last,
The door in the mountain side shut fast.
Did I say all? No! One was lame,
And could not dance the whole of the way;
And in after years, if you would blame
His sadness, he was used to say,—
"It 's dull in our town since my playmates
left!
I can 't forget that I 'm bereft
Of all the pleasant sights they see,
Which the Piper also promised me;
For he led us, he said, to a joyous land,
Joining the town and just at hand,
Where waters gushed and fruit-trees grew,
And flowers put forth a fairer hue,
And every thing was strange and new;
The sparrows were brighter than peacocks
here,
And their dogs outran our fallow deer,
And honey-bees had lost their stings,
And horses were born with eagles' wings;
And just as I became assured
My lame foot would be speedily cured,
The music stopped and I stood still,
And found myself outside the Hill,
Left alone against my will.
To go now limping as before,
And never hear of that country more!"

XIV.

Alas, alas for Hamelin!
There came into many a burgner's pate
A text which says, that Heaven's gate
Opes to the rich at as easy rate
As the needle's eye takes a camel in!
The Mayor sent East, West, North, and
South,
To offer the piper by word of mouth,
Wherever it was men's lot to find him,
Silver and gold to his heart's content,
If he 'd only return the way he went,
And bring the children behind him.
But when they saw 't was a lost endeavor,
And piper and dancers were gone for ever,
They made a decree that lawyers never
Should think their records dated duly
If, after the day of the month and year,
These words did not as well appear,
" And so long after what happened here
On the Twenty-second of July,
Thirteen hundred and Seventy-six;"
And the better in memory to fix
The place of the Children's last retreat
They called it the Pied Piper's Street—
Where any one playing on pipe or tabor
Was sure for the future to lose his labor.
Nor suffered they hostelry or tavern
To shock with mirth a street so solemn;
But opposite the place of the cavern
They wrote the story on a column,
And on the Great Church window painted
The same, to make the world acquainted.
How their children were stolen away;
And there it stands to this very day.
And I must not omit to say
That in Transylvania there 's a tribe
Of alien people that ascribe
The outlandish ways and dress
On which their neighbors lay such stress
To their fathers and mothers having risen
Out of some subterranean prison
Into which they were trepanned
Long time ago, in a mighty band,
Out of Hamelin town in Brunswick land,
But how or why, they do n't understand.

XV.

So, Willy, let you and me be wipers

Of scores out with all men — especially
pipers;
And, whether they pipe us free from rats
or from mice,
If we 've promised them aught, let us keep
our promise.

ROBERT BROWNING.

IVRY.

Now glory to the Lord of hosts, from whom
all glories are!
And glory to our sovereign liege, King
Henry of Navarre!
Now let there be the merry sound of music
and of dance,
Through thy corn-fields green, and sunny
vines, O pleasant land of France!
And thou, Rochelle, our own Rochelle,
proud city of the waters,
Again let rapture light the eyes of all thy
mourning daughters;
As thou wert constant in our ills, be joyous
in our joy;
For cold and stiff and still are they who
wrought thy walls annoy.
Hurrah! hurrah! a single field hath turned
the chance of war!
Hurrah! hurrah! for Ivry, and Henry of
Navarre.

Oh! how our hearts were beating, when, at
the dawn of day,
We saw the army of the league drawn out
in long array;
With all its priest-led citizens, and all its
rebel peers,
And Appenzel's stout infantry, and Eg-
mont's Flemish spears,
There rode the brood of false Lorraine, the
curses of our land;
And dark Mayenne was in the midst, a
truncheon in his hand;
And as we looked on them, we thought of
Seine's empurpled flood,

And good Coligni's hoary hair all dabbled
with his blood;
And we cried unto the living God, who
rules the fate of war,
To fight for His own holy name, and Henry
of Navarre.

The king is come to marshal us, in all his
armor drest;
And he has bound a snow-white plume upon
his gallant crest.
He looked upon his people, and a tear was
in his eye;
He looked upon the traitors, and his glance
was stern and high.
Right graciously he smiled on us, as rolled
from wing to wing,
Down all our line, a deafening shout: God
save our lord the king!
" And if my standard-bearer fall, as fall full
well he may —
For never I saw promise yet of such a
bloody fray —
Press where ye see my white plume shine
amidst the ranks of war,
And be your oriflamme to-day the helmet
of Navarre."

Hurrah! the foes are moving. Hark to
the mingled din,
Of fife, and steed, and trump, and drum,
and roaring culverin.
The fiery duke is pricking fast across Saint
Andre's plain,
With all the hireling chivalry of Guelders
and Almayne.
Now by the lips of those ye love, fair gen-
tlemen of France,
Charge for the golden lilies—upon them
with the lance!
A thousand spurs are striking deep, a thou-
sand spears in rest,
A thousand knights are pressing close
behind the snow-white crest;
And in they burst, and on they rushed,
while, like a guiding star,
Amidst the thickest carnage blazed the hel-
met of Navarre.

Now, God be praised, the day is ours: Mayenne hath turned his rein;
D'Aumale hath cried for quarter; the Flemish count is slain;
Their ranks are breaking like thin clouds
before a Biscay gale;
The field is heaped with bleeding steeds,
and flags, and cloven mail.
And then we thought on vengeance, and,
all along our van,
Remember Saint Bartholomew! was passed
from man to man.
But out spake gentle Henry—"No French-
man is my foe;
Down, down, with every foreigner, but let
your brethren go"—
Oh! was there ever such a knight, in friendship or in war,
As our sovereign lord, King Henry, the
soldier of Navarre?

Right well fought all the Frenchmen who
fought for France to-day;
And many a lordly banner God gave them
for a prey.
But we of the religion have borne us best
in fight;
And the good lord of Rosny hath ta'en the
cornet white—
Our own true Maximilian the cornet white
hath ta'en,
The cornet white with crosses black, the
flag of false Lorraine.
Up with it high; unfurl it wide—that all
the host may know
How God hath humbled the proud house
which wrought His Church such woe.
Then on the ground, while trumpets sound
their loudest point of war,
Fling the red shreds, a footcloth meet for
Henry of Navarre.

Ho! maidens of Vienna; ho! matrons of
Lucerne—
Weep, weep, and rend your hair for those
who never shall return.
Ho! Philip, send, for charity, thy Mexican
pistoles,

That Antwerp monks may sing a mass for
thy poor spearmen's souls.
Ho! gallant nobles of the league, look that
your arms be bright;
Ho! burghers of St. Genevieve, keep watch
and ward to-night;
For our God hath crushed the tyrant, our
God hath raised the slave,
And mocked the counsel of the wise, and
the valor of the brave.
Then glory to His holy name, from whom
all glories are;
And glory to our sovereign lord, King
Henry of Navarre!

Lord Macaulay.

RED AND WHITE.

Under the trees by the darkling stream
The red chief lurks at morning;
His dusk cheek flushes—an angry gleam
Is in his wild eye—scorning
All food or sleep, in a vengeful dream
He waits for the scout's shrill warning.

The sun rides high, and the forest screen
Is pierced, and the sluggish river
Lights up and laughs, and the murky green
Grows cool with a golden shiver—
But the red chief whetteth his knife so keen
And loosens the store of his quiver.

Down sinks the sun, the evening hymn
Of birds to heaven hath risen;
All in the stillness that chief so grim
He springs to his feet to listen,
And the red men crouch by the river's brim
With hungry eyes that glisten.

There's a plashing of oars in the turbid
wave,
There's a glitter of knives in the brake,
With a careless boat-song on to their grave,
With the dying sun in their wake,
The robbers come, who have roused the
brave
A sudden revenge to take.

RED AND WHITE,

The men who dreamed that the dusky
   maids
Should smile in the huts of the pale—
O, long shall their daughters through forest
   glades
Gaze out, and their wives shall wail,
For keen and sure are the red men's blades,
   And the river tells no tale.

B. MONTGOMERIE RANKING.

THE DEVIL'S THOUGHTS.

I.

FROM his brimstone bed at break of day
A walking the devil is gone,
To visit his snug little farm, the earth,
   And see how his stock goes on.

II.

Over the hill and over the dale,
   And he went over the plain;
And backward and forward he switched his
   long tail,
   As a gentleman switches his cane.

III.

And how then was the devil drest?
Oh! he was in his Sunday's best:
His jacket was red and his breeches were
   blue,
And there was a hole where the tail came
   through.

IV.

He saw a lawyer killing a viper
   On a dunghill hard by his own stable;
And the devil smiled, for it put him in
   mind
   Of Cain and his brother Abel.

V.

He saw an apothecary on a white horse
   Ride by on his vocations;
And the devil thought of his old friend
   Death, in the Revelations.

VI.

He saw a cottage with a double coach-house
   A cottage of gentility;
And the devil did grin, for his darling sin
   Is pride that apes humility.

VII.

He peeped into a rich bookseller's shop—
   Quoth he, "We are both of one college!
For I sate, myself, like a cormorant, once,
   Hard by the tree of knowledge."

VIII.

Down the river did glide, with wind and
   with tide,
   A pig with vast celerity;
And the devil looked wise as he saw how,
   the while,
It cut its own throat. "There!" quoth he
   with a smile,
"Goes England's commercial prosperity."

IX.

As he went through Cold-Bath Fields he saw
   A solitary cell;
And the devil was pleased, for it gave him
   a hint
   For improving his prisons in hell.

X.

He saw a turnkey in a trice
   Fetter a troublesome blade;
"Nimbly," quoth he, "do the fingers move
   If a man be but used to his trade."

XI.

He saw the same turnkey unfetter a man
   With but little expedition;
Which put him in mind of the long debate
   On the slave-trade abolition.

XII.

He saw an old acquaintance
   As he passed by a Methodist meeting;
She holds a consecrated key,
   And the devil nods her a greeting.

XIII.

She turned up her nose, and said,
  "Avaunt!—my name 's Religion!"
And she looked to Mr. ——,
  And leered like a love-sick pigeon.

XIV.

He saw a certain minister,
  A minister to his mind,
Go up into a certain house,
  With a majority behind;

XV.

The devil quoted Genesis,
  Like a very learned clerk,
How " Noah and his creeping things
  Went up into the ark."

XVI.

He took from the poor,
  And he gave to the rich,
And he shook hands with a Scotchman,
  For he was not afraid of the ——
    *   *   *   *

XVII.

General —————— burning face
  He saw with consternation,
And back to hell his way did he take—
  For the devil thought by a slight mistake
It was a general conflagration.
             SAMUEL TAYLOR COLERIDGE.

———

SWEET SUMMER TIME.

WHO has not dreamed a world of bliss
On a bright sunny noon like this,
Couched by his native brook's green maze,
With comrade of his boyish days,
While all around them seemed to be
Just as in joyous infancy;
Who has not loved at such an hour,
Upon that heath in birchen bower,
Lu.. d in the poet's dreamy mood,
Its wild and sunny solitude?

While o'er the waste of purple ling
You mark a sultry glimmering;
Silence herself there seems to sleep,
Wrapped in a slumber long and deep,
Where slowly stray those lonely sheep
Through the tall foxglove's crimson bloom,
And gleaming of the scattered broom,
Love you not, then, to list and hear
The crackling of the gorse-flowers near,
Pouring an orange-scented tide
Of fragrance o'er the desert wide?
To hear the buzzard's whimpering shrill,
Hovering above you high and still?
The twittering of the bird that dwells
Among the heath's delicious bells?
While round your bed, o'er fern and blade,
Insects in green and gold arrayed,
The sun's gay tribes have lightly strayed;
And sweeter sound their humming wings
Than the proud minstrel's echoing strings.
             WILLIAM HOWITT.

———

TAM O'SHANTER.

A TALE.

Of Brownyis and of Bogilis full is this Buke.
               Gawin Douglass.

WHEN chapman billies leave the street,
And drouthy neebors neebors meet,
As market-days are wearing late,
An' folk begin to tak the gate;
While we sit bousing at the nappy,
An' getting fou and unco happy,
We think na on the lang Scots miles,
The mosses, waters, slaps, and styles,
That lie between us and our hame,
Whare sits our sulky, sullen dame,
Gathering her brows like gathering storm,
Nursing her wrath to keep it warm.
  This truth fand honest Tam o' Shanter,
As he, frae Ayr, ae night did canter,
(Auld Ayr, wham ne'er a town surpasses,
For honest men and bonnie lasses).
  O Tam! hadst thou been but sae wise
As taen thy ain wife Kate's advice!
She tauld thee weel thou was a skellum,
A bleth'ring, blust'ring, drunken blellum,

That frae November till October,
Ae market-day thou was na sober;
That ilka melder, wi' the miller,
Thou sat as lang as thou had siller;
That every naig was ca'd a shoe on,
The smith and thee gat roaring fou on;
That at the L—d's house, ev'n on Sunday,
Thou drank wi' Kirten Jean till Monday.
She prophesied that, late or soon,
Thou would be found deep drowned in
    Doon;
Or catched wi' warlocks in the mirk,
By Alloway's auld haunted kirk.

Ah, gentle dames! it gars me greet
To think how monie counsels sweet,
How monie lengthened sage advices,
The husband frae the wife despises!

But to our tale: Ae market night
Tam had got planted unco right,
Fast by an ingle, bleezing finely,
Wi' reaming swats, that drank divinely;
And at his elbow souter Johnny,
His ancient, trusty, drouthy crony—
Tam lo'ed him like a vera brither—
They had been fou for weeks thegither,
The night drave on wi' sangs and clatter,
And ay the ale was growing better;
The landlady and Tam grew gracious,
Wi' favors secret, sweet, and precious;
The souter tauld his queerest stories;
The landlord's laugh was ready chorus;
The storm without might rair and rustle,
Tam did na mind the storm a whistle.

Care, mad to see a man sae happy,
E'en drowned himself amang the nappy;
As bees flee hame wi' lades o' treasure,
The minutes winged their way wi' pleasure;
Kings may be blest, but Tam was glorious,
O'er a' the ills o' life victorious.

But pleasures are like poppies spread,
You seize the flower, its bloom is shed;
Or like the snow-fall in the river,
A moment white—then melts forever;
Or like the borealis race,
That flit ere you can point their place;
Or like the rainbow's lovely form
Evanishing amid the storm.
Nae man can tether time or tide;
The hour approaches Tam maun ride—

That hour o' night's black arch the keystane,
That dreary hour he mounts his beast in;
And sic a night he takes the road in
As ne'er poor sinner was abroad in.

The wind blew as 'twad blawn its last;
The rattling showers rose on the blast;
The speedy gleams the darkness swallowed;
Loud, deep, and lang, the thunder bellowed;
That night a child might understand
The Deil had business on his hand.

Weel mounted on his gray mare, Meg,
(A better never lifted leg),
Tam skelpit on thro' dub and mire,
Despising wind, and rain, and fire—
Whyles holding fast his guid blue bonnet,
Whyles crooning o'er some auld Scots
    sonnet,
Whyles glow'ring round wi' prudent cares,
Lest bogles catch him unawares;
Kirk-Alloway was drawing nigh,
Where ghaists and houlets nightly cry.

By this time he was cross the ford,
Where in the snaw the chapman smoored;
And past the birks and meikle stane,
Whare drunken Charlie brak 's neck bane;
And thro' the whins, and by the cairn,
Whare hunters fand the murdered bairn;
And near the thorn, aboon the well,
Where Mungo's mither hanged hersel.
Before him Doon pours all his floods;
The doubling storm roars through the
    . woods;
The lightnings flash from pole to pole;
Near and more near the thunders roll;
When glimmering thro' the groaning trees,
Kirk Alloway seemed in a bleeze;
Thro' ilka bore the beams were glancing,
And loud resounded mirth and dancing,
    Inspiring bold John Barleycorn!
What dangers thou can'st make us scorn!
Wi' tippenny we fear nae evil;
Wi' usquabae we 'll face the Devil!
The swats sae ream'd in Tammie's noddle,
Fair play, he cared na Deils a bodle.
But Maggie stood right sair astonished,
Till, by the heel and hand admonished,
She ventured forward on the light;
And, wow! Tam saw an unco sight;
Warlocks and witches in a dance;

Nae cotillion brent new frae France,
But hornpipes, jigs, strathspreys, and reels
Put life and mettle in their heels.
A winnock-bunker in the east,
There sat auld Nick, in shape o' beast—
A towzie tyke, black, grim, and large—
To gie them music was his charge;
He screwed the pipes and gart them skirl,
Till roof an' rafter a' did dirl.
Coffins stood round like open presses,
That shawed the dead in their last dresses;
And by some devilish cantrips sleight,
Each in its cauld hand held a light—
By which heroic Tam was able
To note upon the haly table,
A murderer's banes in gibbet airns;
Twa span-lang, wee, unchristened bairns;
A thief, new cutted fra a rape,
Wi' his last gasp his gab did gape;
Five tomahawks, wi' bluid red rusted;
Five scymitars, wi' murder crusted;
A garter which a babe had strangled;
A knife a father's throat had mangled,
Whom his ain son o' life bereft—
The gray hairs yet stack to the heft;
Three lawyers' tongues turned inside out,
Wi' lies seamed like a beggar's clout;
And priests' hearts, rotten, black as muck,
Lay stinking, vile, in every neuk:
Wi' mair o' horrible and awfu'
Which ev'n to name would be unlawfu'.
   As Tammie glowred, amazed, and curious,
The mirth and fun grew fast and furious:
The piper loud and louder blew;
The dancers quick and quicker flew;
They reeled, they set, they crossed, they cleckit,
Till ilka carlin swat and reekit,
And coost her duddies to the wark,
And linket at it in her sark.
   Now Tam, O Tam! had they been queans,
A' plump and strapping in their teens;
Their sarks, instead of creeshie flannen,
Been snaw-white seventeen-hunder linen;
Thir breeks o' mine, my only pair,
That ance were plush, o' guid blue hair,
I wad hae gi'en them aff my hurdies,
For ae blink o' the bonnie burdies!
   But withered beldams, auld and droll,
Rigwoodie hags, wad spean a foal,

Lowping an' flinging on a crummock—
I wonder did na turn thy stomach.
   But Tam kenn'd what was what fu' brawlie,
There was ae winsome wench and walie,
That night enlisted in the core,
(Lang after kenn'd on Carrick shore!
For monie a beast to dead she shot,
And perished monie a bonnie boat,
And shook baith meikle corn and bear,
And kept the country-side in fear),
Her cutty-sark o' Paisley harn,
That while a lassie she had worn—
In longitude tho' sorely scanty,
It was her best, and she was vaunty.
Ah! little kenn'd thy reverend grannie
That sark she coft for her wee Nannie,
Wi' twa pund Scots (twas a' her riches)—
Wad ever graced a dance o' witches!
   But here my Muse her wing maun cower,
Sic flights are far beyond her power;
To sing how Nannie lap and flang,
(A souple jad she was and strang);
And how Tam stood, like ane bewitched,
And thought his very een enriched.
Ev'n Satan glowred, and fidged fu' fain,
And hotched and blew wi' might and main
Till first ae caper, syne anither—
Tam tint his reason a' thegither,
And roars out, "Weel done, Cutty-sark!"
And in an instant a' was dark;
And scarcely had he Maggie rallied,
When out the hellish legion sallied,
   As bees bizz out wi' angry fyke,
When plundering herds assail their byke;
As open pussie's mortal foes,
When pop! she starts before their nose;
As eager runs the market-crowd,
When *Catch the thief!* resounds aloud;
So Maggie runs—the witches follow,
Wi' monie an eldritch skreech and hollow.
   Ah, Tam! ah, Tam! thou'll get thy fairin'!
In hell they'll roast thee like a herrin!
In vain thy Kate awaits thy comin'—
Kate soon will be a woefu' woman!
Now, do thy speedy utmost, Meg,
And win the key-stane of the brig;
There at them thou thy tail may toss—
A running stream they dare na cross.

But ere the key-stane she could make,
The fient a tail she had to shake;
For Nannie, far before the rest,
Hard upon noble Maggie prest,
And flew at Tam wi' furious ettle:
But little wist she Maggie's mettle—
Ae spring brought aff her master hale,
But left behind her ain gray tail:
The carlin claught her by the rump,
And left poor Maggie scarce a stump.

Now, wha this tale o' truth shall read,
Ilk man and mother's son take heed;
Whene'er to drink you are inclined,
Or cutty-sarks run in your mind,
Think, ye may buy the joys o'er dear,
Remember Tam o' Shanter's mare.

ROBERT BURNS.

HYMN

BEFORE SUNRISE, IN THE VALE OF CHAMOUNI.

HAST thou a charm to stay the morning-star
In his steep course? So long he seems to
    pause
On thy bald, awful head, O sovereign Blanc!
The Arve and Arveiron at thy base
Rave ceaselessly; but thou, most awful
    Form,
Risest from forth thy silent sea of pines,
How silently! Around thee and above
Deep is the air and dark, substantial,
    black—
An ebon mass. Methinks thou piercest it,
As with a wedge! But when I look again,
It is thine own calm home, thy crystal
    shrine,
Thy habitation from eternity!
O dread and silent Mount! I gazed upon
    thee,
Till thou, still present to the bodily sense,
Didst vanish from my thought. Entranced
    in prayer
I worshipped the Invisible alone.

Yet, like some sweet beguiling melody,
So sweet we know not we are listening to it,

Thou, the meanwhile, wast blending with
    my thought—
Yea, with my life and life's own secret joy—
Till the dilating soul, enrapt, transfused,
Into the mighty vision passing—there,
As in her natural form, swelled vast to
    Heaven!

Awake, my soul! not only passive praise
Thou owest! not alone these swelling tears,
Mute thanks and secret ectasy! Awake,
Voice of sweet song! Awake, my heart,
    awake!
Green vales and icy cliffs, all join my
    hymn.
    Thou first and chief, sole sovereign of
        the vale!
Oh, struggling with the darkness all the
    night,
And visited all night by troops of stars,
Or when they climb the sky or when they
    sink—
Companion of the morning-star at dawn,
Thyself Earth's rosy star, and of the dawn
Co-herald — wake, oh wake, and utter
    praise!
Who sank thy sunless pillars deep in earth?
Who filled thy countenance with rosy light?
Who made thee parent of perpetual
    streams?

    And you, ye five wild torrents fiercely
        glad!
Who called you forth from night and utter
    death,
From dark and icy caverns called you forth,
Down those precipitous, black, jagged
    rocks,
For ever shattered and the same for ever?
Who gave you your invulnerable life,
Your strength, your speed, your fury, and
    your joy,
Unceasing thunder and eternal foam?
And who commanded (and the silence
    came),
Here let the billows stiffen, and have rest?

    Ye ice-falls! ye that from the mountain's
        brow
Adown enormous ravines slope amain—

Torrents, methinks, that heard a mighty
  voice,
And stopped at once amid their maddest
  plunge!
Motionless torrents! silent cataracts!
Who made you g'orious as the gates of
  Heaven
Beneath the keen full moon? Who bade
  the sun ,
Clothe you with rainbows? Who, with liv-
  ing flowers
Of lovliest blue, spread garlands at your
  feet?
God!—let the torrents, like a shout of na-
  tions,
Answer! and let the ice-plains echo, God!
God! sing ye meadow-streams with glad-
  some voice!
Ye pine-groves, with your soft and soul-like
  sounds!
And they too have a voice, yon piles of snow,
And in their perilous fall shall thunder,
  God!
  Ye living flowers that skirt the eternal
  frost!
Ye wild goats sporting round the eagle's
  'nest!
Ye eagles, playmates of the mountain-
  storm!
Ye lightnings, the dread arrows of the
  clouds!
Ye signs and wonders of the elements!
Utter forth God, and fill the hills with
  praise!

Thou too, hoar Mount! with thy sky-
  pointing peaks,
Oft from whose feet the avalanche unheard,
Shoots downward, glittering through the
  pure serene,
Into the depths of clouds that veil thy
  breast—
Thou too again, stupendous Mountain! thou
That as I raise my head, awhile bowed low
In adoration, upward from thy base
Slow travelling with dim eyes suffused
  with tears,
Solemnly seemest, like a vapory cloud,
To rise before me—Rise, oh ever rise!

Rise like a cloud of incense, from the
  Earth!
Thou kingly Spirit throned among the hills,
Thou dread ambassador from Earth to
  Heaven,
Great Hierarch! tell thou the silent sky,
And tell the stars, and tell yon rising sun,
Earth, with her thousand voices, praises
  God.
  SAMUEL TAYLOR COLERIDGE.

BLIGHTED LOVE.

----

*(From the Portuguese of Luis De Camoens, by
Lord Strangford.)*

FLOWERS are fresh, and bushes green,
  Cheerily the linnets sing;
Winds are soft, and skies serene;
  Time, however, soon shall throw
    Winter's snow
  O'er the buxom breast of spring!

Hope, that buds in lover's heart,
  Lives not through the scorn of years;
Time makes love itself depart;
  Time and storm congeal the mind,—
    Looks unkind,
  Freeze affection's warmest tears.

Time shall make the bushes green;
  Time dissolve the winter's snow;
Winds be soft, and skies serene;
  Linnets sing their wonted strain:
    But again
  Blighted love shall never blow

MAUD MULLER.

MAUD MULLER, on a summer's day,
Raked the meadow sweet with hay.

Beneath her torn hat glowed the wealth
Of simple beauty and rustic health.

BLIGHTED LOVE.

Singing, she wrought, and her merry glee
The mock-bird echoed from his tree.

But, when she glanced to the far-off town,
White from its hill-slope looking down,

The sweet song died, and a vague unrest
And a nameless longing filled her breast—

A wish, that she hardly dared to own,
For something better than she had known.

The judge rode slowly down the lane,
Smoothing his horse's chestnut mane.

He drew his bridle in the shade
Of the apple-trees, to greet the maid,

And ask a draught from the spring that flowed
Through the meadow, across the road.

She stooped where the cool spring bubbled up,
And filled for him her small tin cup,

And blushed as she gave it, looking down
On her feet so bare, and her tattered gown.

"Thanks!" said the judge, "a sweeter draught
From a fairer hand was never quaffed."

He spoke of the grass and flowers and trees,
Of the singing birds and the humming bees;

Then talked of the haying, and wondered whether
The cloud in the west would bring foul weather.

And Maud forgot her brier-torn gown,
And her graceful ankles, bare and brown,

And listened, while a pleased surprise
Looked from her long-lashed hazel-eyes.

At last, like one who for delay
Seeks a vain excuse, he rode away.

Maud Muller looked and sighed: "Ah me!
That I the judge's bride might be!

"He would dress me up in silks so fine,
And praise and toast me at his wine.

"My father should wear a broadcloth coat,
My brother should sail a painted boat.

"I'd dress my mother so grand and gay,
And the baby should have a new toy each day.

"And I'd feed the hungry and clothe the poor,
And all should bless me who left our door."

The judge looked back as he climbed the hill,
And saw Maud Muller standing still:

"A form more fair, a face more sweet,
Ne'er hath it been my lot to meet.

"And her modest answer and graceful air
Show her wise and good as she is fair.

"Would she were mine, and I to-day,
Like her, a harvester of hay.

"No doubtful balance of rights and wrongs,
Nor weary lawyers with endless tongues,

"But low of cattle, and song of birds,
And health, and quiet, and loving words."

But he thought of his sister, proud and cold,
And his mother, vain of her rank and gold.

So, closing his heart, the judge rode on,
And Maud was left in the field alone.

But the lawyers smiled that afternoon,
When he hummed in court an old love tune:

And the young girl mused beside the well,
Till the rain on the unraked clover fell.

He wedded a wife of richest dower,
Who lived for fashion, as he for power.

Yet oft, in his marble hearth's bright glow,
He watched a picture come and go;

And sweet Maud Muller's hazel eyes
Looked out in their innocent surprise.

Oft, when the wine in his glass was red,
He longed for the wayside well instead,

And closed his eyes on his garnished rooms,
To dream of meadows and clover blooms;

And the proud man sighed with a secret
    pain,
" Ah, that I were free again!

" Free as when I rode that day
Where the barefoot maiden raked the hay."

She wedded a man unlearned and poor,
And many children played round her door.

But care and sorrow, and child-birth pain,
Left their traces on heart and brain.

And oft, when the summer sun shone hot
On the new-mown hay in the meadow lot,

And she heard the little spring brook fall
Over the roadside, through the wall,

In the shade of the apple-tree again
She saw a rider draw his rein,

And, gazing down with a timid grace,
She felt his pleased eyes read her face.

Sometimes her narrow kitchen walls
Stretched away into stately halls;

The weary wheel to a spinnet turned,
The tallow candle an astral burned;

And for him who sat by the chimney lug,
Dozing and grumbling o'er pipe and mug,

A manly form at her side she saw,
And joy was duty and love was law.

Then she took up her burden of life again,
Saying only, " It might have been."

Alas for maiden, alas for judge,
For rich repiner and household drudge!

God pity them both! and pity us all,
Who vainly the dreams of youth recall;

For of all sad words of tongue or pen,
The saddest are these: " It might have
    been!"

Ah, well! for us all some sweet hope lies
Deeply buried from human eyes;

And, in the hereafter, angels may
Roll the stone from his grave away! .
    JOHN GREENLEAF WHITTIER.

WE PARTED IN SILENCE.

WE parted in silence, we parted by night,
    On the banks of that lonely river;
Where the fragrant limes their boughs
    unite.
    We met—and we parted forever!
The night-bird sung—and the stars above
    Told many a touching story
Of friends long passed to the kingdom of
    love,
    Where the soul wears its mantle of glory.

We parted in silence,—our cheeks were wet
    With the tears that were past controlling;
We vowed we would never, no, never
    forget,
    And those vows at the time were con-
        soling;
But those lips that echoed the sounds of
    mine
    Are as cold as that lonely river;
And that eye, that beautiful spirit's shrine,
    Has shrouded its fires forever.

WE PARTED IN SILENCE.

And now on the midnight sky I look,
  And my heart grows full of weeping;
Each star is to me a sealed book,
  Some tale of that loved one keeping.
We parted in silence,—we parted in tears
  On the banks of that lonely river;
But the odor and bloom of those bygone
    years
  Shall hang o'er its waters forever.
                    —MRS. CRAWFORD.

ANNIE LAURIE.

MAXWELTON braes are bonnie
  Where early fa's the dew,
And it 's there that Annie Laurie
  Gie'd me her promise true;
Gie'd me her promise true,
  Which ne'er forgot will be;
And for bonnie Annie Laurie
  I 'd lay me doune and dee.

Her brow is like the snaw drift;
  Her throat is like the swan;
Her face it is the fairest
  That e'er the sun shone on—
That e'er the sun shone on—
  And dark blue is her ee;
And for bonnie Annie Laurie
  I 'd lay me doune and dee.

Like dew on the gowan lying
  Is the fa' o' her fairy feet;
And like the winds in summer sighing,
  Her voice is low and sweet—
Her voice is low and sweet—
  And she 's a' the world to me;
And for bonnie Annie Laurie
  I 'd lay me doune and dee.
                    ANONYMOUS.

THE IVY GREEN.

OH! a dainty plant is the Ivy green,
  That creepeth o'er ruins old!
Of right choice food are his meals I ween,
  In his cell so lone and cold.

The walls must be crumbled, the stones
    decayed,
  To pleasure his dainty whim;
And the mouldering dust that years have
    made
  Is a merry meal for him.
      Creeping where no life is seen,
      A rare old plant is the Ivy green.
Fast he stealeth on, though he wears no
    wings,
  And a staunch old heart has he!
How closely he twineth, how tight he clings
  To his friend, the huge oak tree!
And slyly he traileth along the ground,
  And his leaves he gently waves,
And he joyously twines and hugs around
  The rich mould of dead men's graves.
      Creeping where no life is seen,
      A rare old plant is the Ivy green.

Whole ages have fled, and their works de-
    cayed,
  And nations scattered been;
But the stout old Ivy shall never fade
  From its hale and hearty green.
The brave old plant in its lonely days
  Shall fatten upon the past;
For the stateliest building man can raise
  Is the Ivy's food at last.
      Creeping where no life is seen,
      A rare old plant is the Ivy green.
                    CHARLES DICKENS.

AMID THE ROSES.

I SEEK her midst the roses, and
  My soul is sore for love.
Her image beams serenely grand
  As Cynthia's form above,
Enchas'd in halo. Brave my hand
  To grasp thy treasure trove!

I seek her midst the roses, for
  I may no longer wait
A suitor reckless at her door,
  And flinch to learn my fate.
I dare not hope. I dare no more
  Than humbly supplicate.

I seek her midst the roses, where
  Soft pleasures, redolent
Of gracious things, enrich the air
  Impregnate with their scent.
She can but choose to hear a prayer
  With odor thus besprent.

I meet her midst the roses. Yes;
  Hard by the mossy briars.
One bud she clasps in close caress,
  So cold, though near her fires.
To live as that, nor more nor less,
  Would surfeit Jove's desires.

I greet her midst the roses, while
  Fierce burns the breath of May.
Why turns she to avoid my smile?
  Why cast her bud away?
Just Phœbus! could a thing of guile
  Deserve a darker day?

Yet, no! Amid the roses, I
  Will deem her cruel-kind:
When maiden frowns disdainfully
  'T were wisdom to be blind.
'T were weak to count a wilful eye
  The reflex of her mind.

Thus, tremulous midst the roses, lest
  My love its love should miss,
I falter forth a bold request
  That she will grant me bliss—
But once to sip her best of best,
  The nectar of a kiss.

She midst her roses stands apart
  In silvern panoply
Of innocence. But Cupid's dart,
  Though fitted warily,
Wings not its flight. Must I depart
  Shamed of my urgency?

Ye roses! "Such request, Sir Knight
  Fond heart should never rue."
I hear a whisper, laughing light,
  "Though best of best for you,
Nor coral lip, nor forehead white,
  Rather this silken shoe!"

An echo from the roses rends
  My bosom and the sky.
Humbly I kneel. My right hand bends
  Her latchet to untie,
Whilst she a dainty foot extends
  In gesture mockingly.

Then mid the blossoms ruby red
  The Boy-God draws his shaft.
Home has the love-tipt arrow sped
  On roseate odors waft.
She thrills. Her dainty heart has bled
  Ere my poor lips have quaffed.

In true obeisance hers, not her,
  The fire-containing ice.
No cause to cringe, no fear to err;
  She changes in a trice
From white to rose; confessing, "Sir,
  You give me Paradise."

Ye swains, amid the roses find
  'T were wisdom to be true.
Your Chloe's test may seem unkind,
  And hard your Chloe's shoe;
Yet when she proves your constant mind
  She 'll e'en consent to you.
                    —COMPTON READE.

THE KITTEN AND FALLING LEAVES.

THAT way look, my infant, lo!
What a pretty baby-show!
See the kitten on the wall,
Sporting with the leaves that fall—
Withered leaves,—one, two, and three,—
From the lofty elder tree!
Through the calm and frosty air
Of this morning bright and fair,
Eddying round and round, they sink
Softly, slowly; one might think,
From the motions that are made,
Every little leaf conveyed
Sylph or fairy hither tending,
To this lower world descending,

AMID THE ROSES.

Each invisible and mute
In his wavering parachute.
—— But the Kitten, how she starts,
Crouches, stretches, paws, and darts!
First at one, and then its fellow
Just as light and just as yellow;
There are many now,—now one,—
Now they stop, and there are none.
What intenseness of desire
In her upward eye of fire!
With a tiger-leap! Half-way
Now she meets the coming prey,
Lets it go as fast, and then
Has it in her power again;
Now she works with three or four,
Like an Indian conjurer;
Quick as he in feats of art,
Far beyond in joy of heart.
Were her antics played in the eye
Of a thousand standers-by,
Clapping hands with shout and stare,
What would little Tabby care
For the plaudits of the crowd?
Over happy to be proud,
Over wealthy in the treasure
Of her own exceeding pleasure!

'T is a pretty baby treat,
Nor, I deem, for me unmeet;
Here for neither Babe nor me
Other playmate can I see.
Of the countless living things
That with stir of feet and wings
(In the sun or under shade,
Upon bough or grassy blade),
And with busy revellings,
Chirp, and song, and murmurings,
Made this orchard's narrow space,
And this vale, so blithe a place;
Multitudes are swept away,
Never more to breathe the day.
Some are sleeping; some in bands
Travelled into distant lands;
Others slunk to moor and wood,
Far from human neighborhood;
And, among the kinds that keep
With us closer fellowship,
With us openly abide,
All have laid their mirth aside.

Where is he, that giddy sprite,
Blue-cap, with his colors bright,
Who was blest as bird could be,
Feeding in the apple-tree—
Made such wanton spoil and rout,
Turning blossoms inside out—
Hung, head pointing towards the ground,
Fluttered, perched, into a round
Bound himself, and then unbound—
Lithest, gaudiest Harlequin!
Prettiest tumbler ever seen!
Light of heart, and light of limb—
What is now become of him?
Lambs, that through the mountains went
Frisking, bleating merriment,
When the year was in its prime,
They are sobered by this time.
If you look to vale or hill,
If you listen, all is still,
Save a little neighboring rill
That from out the rocky ground
Strikes a solitary sound.
Vainly glitter hill and plain,
And the air is calm in vain;
Vainly Morning spreads the lure
Of a sky serene and pure;
Creature none can she decoy
Into open sign of joy.
Is it that they have a fear
Of the dreary season near?
Or that other pleasures be
Sweeter even than gayety?

Yet, whate'er enjoyments dwell
In the impenetrable cell
Of the silent heart which Nature
Furnishes to every creature—
Whatsoe'er we feel and know
Too sedate for outward show—
Such a light of gladness breaks,
Pretty Kitten! from thy freaks,—
Spreads with such a living grace
O'er my little Dora's face—
Yes, the sight so stirs and charms
Thee, Baby, laughing in my arms,
That almost I could repine
That your transports are not mine,
That I do not wholly fare
Even as ye do, thoughtless pair!

And I will have my careless season
Spite of melancholy reason,
Will walk through life in such a way
That, when time brings on decay,
Now and then I may possess
Hours of perfect gladsomeness.
Pleased by any random toy—
By a kitten's busy joy,
Or an infant's laughing eye
Sharing the ecstasy—
I would fare like that or this,
Find my wisdom in my bliss,
Keep the sprightly soul awake,
And have faculties to take,
Even from things by sorrow wrought,
Matter for a jocund thought—
Spite of care, and spite of grief,
To gambol with Life's falling leaf.

           WILLIAM WORDSWORTH.

MARY MORISON.

O, MARY, at thy window be,
   It is the wished, the trysted hour,
Those smiles and glances let me see,
   That make the miser's treasure poor.
How blithely wad I bide the stoure,
   A weary slave frae sun to sun,
Could I the rich reward secure,
   The lovely Mary Morison.

Yestreen, when to the trembling string
   The dance gaed through the lighted ha',
To thee my fancy took its wing,
   I sat, but neither heard nor saw;
Though this was fair, and that was braw,
   And you the toast of a' the town,
I sighed, and said amang them a',
   "Ye are na Mary Morison!"

Oh, Mary! canst thou wreck his peace,
   Wha for thy sake wad gladly dee?
Or canst thou break that heart of his,
   Whose only fault is loving thee?
If love for love thou wilt na gie,
   At least be pity to me shown!
A thought ungentle canna be
   The thought o' Mary Morison.

           ROBERT BURNS.

THE CHILD AND THE WATCHER.

SLEEP on, baby on the floor,
   Tired of all thy playing—
Sleep on with smile the sweeter for
   That you dropped away in;
On your curls' fair roundness stand
   Golden lights serenely;
One cheek, pushed out by the hand,
   Folds the dimple inly—
Little head and little foot
   Heavy laid for pleasure;
Underneath the lids half-shut
   Plants the shining azure;
Open-souled in noonday sun,
   So, you lie and slumber;
Nothing evil having done,
   Nothing can encumber.

I, who cannot sleep as well,
   Shall I sigh to view you?
Or sigh further to foretell
   All that may undo you?
Nay, keep smiling, little child,
   Ere the faith appeareth!
I smile, too; for patience mild
   Pleasure's token weareth.
Nay, keep sleeping before loss;
   I shall sleep, though losing!
As by cradle, so by cross,
   Sweet is the reposing.

And God knows, who sees us twain,
   Child at childish leisure,
I am all as tired of pain
   As you are of pleasure.
Very soon, too, by His grace,
   Gently wrapt around me,
I shall show as calm a face,
   I shall sleep as soundly—
Differing in this, that you
   Clasp your playthings sleeping,
While my hand must drop the few
   Given to my keeping—

Differing in this, that I,
   Sleeping, must be colder,
And in waking presently,
   Brighter to beholder—

MARY MORRISON.

Differing in this beside
(Sleeper, have you heard me?)
Do you move, and open wide
Your great eyes toward me?)
That while I you draw withal
From this slumber solely,
Me, from mine, an angel shall,
Trumpet-tongued and holy!
ELIZABETH BARRETT BROWNING.

LOCHINVAR.

Oh, young Lochinvar is come out of the
west;
Through all the wide border his steed was
the best;
And save his good broad-sword he weapons
had none;
He rode all unarmed, and he rode all alone.
So faithful in love and so dauntless in war,
There never was knight like the young
Lochinvar.

He staid not for brake, and he stopped not
for stone;
He swam the Eske river where ford there
was none;
But, ere he alighted at Netherby gate,
The bride had consented, the gallant came
late;
For a laggard in love and a dastard in war,
Was to wed the fair Ellen of brave Loch-
invar.

So boldly he entered the Netherby hall,
'Mong bridesmen, and kinsmen, and broth-
ers, and all;
Then spoke the bride's father, his hand on
his sword,
(For the poor craven bridegroom said never
a word,)
" Oh come ye in peace here, or come ye in
war,
Or to dance at our bridal, young Lord
Lochinvar?"

" I long wooed your daughter, my suit you
denied—

Love swells like the Solway, but ebbs like
its tide—
And now I am come, with this lost love of
mine,
To lead but one measure, drink one cup of
wine;
There are maidens in Scotland more lovely
by far,
That would gladly be bride to the young
Lochinvar."

The bride kissed the goblet—the knight
took it up;
He quaffed off the wine. and he threw down
the cup.
She looked down to blush, and she looked
up to sigh,
With a smile on her lips and a tear in her
eye.
He took her soft hand, ere her mother
could bar,—
"Now tread we a measure!" said young
Lochinvar.

So stately his form, and so lovely her face,
That never a hall such a galliard did grace;
While her mother did fret and her father
did fume,
And the bridegroom stood dangling his
bonnet and plume;
And the bride-maidens whispered, "'T were
better by far
To have matched our fair cousin with
young Lochinvar."

One touch to her hand, and one word in
her ear,
When they reached the hall door and the
charger stood near;
So light to the croupe the fair lady he swung
So light to the saddle before her he sprung!
"She is won! we are gone, over bank, bush,
and scaur;
They'll have fleet steeds that follow," quoth young Lochinvar.

There was mounting 'mong Græmes of the
Netherby clan;

Forsters, Fenwicks, and Musgraves, they
　　rode and they ran:
There was racing, and chasing, on Canno-
　　bie Lee,
But the lost bride of Netherby ne'er did
　　they see.
So daring in love, and so dauntless in war,
Have ye e'er heard of gallant like young
　　Lochinvar?
SIR WALTER SCOTT.

MAY.

May, thou month of rosy beauty,
Month when pleasure is a duty;
Month of maids that milk the kine,
Bosom rich, and health divine;
Month of bees and month of flowers,
Month of blossom-laden bowers;
Month of little hands with daisies,
Lover's love, and poet's praises;
O thou merry month complete,
May, the very name is sweet!
May was MAID in olden times—
And is still in Scottish rhymes—
May's the month that's laughing now.
I no sooner write the word,
Than it seems as though it heard,
And looks up and laughs at me,
Like a sweet face, rosily,—
Flushing from the paper's white;
Like a bride that knows her power
Startled in a summer bower.

If the rains that do us wrong
Come to keep the winter long
And deny us thy sweet looks,
I can love thee, sweet, in books;
Love thee in the poet's pages,
Where they keep thee green for ages;
Love and read thee as a lover
Reads his lady's letter over,
Breathing blessings on the art
Which commingles those that part.
There is May in books for ever:
May will part from Spencer never;
May's in Milton, May's in Prior,
May's in Chaucer, Thomson, Dyer;

May's in all the Italian books;
She has old and modern nooks,
Where she sleeps with nymphs and elves,
In happy places they call shelves,
And will rise and dress your rooms
With a drapery thick with blooms.

Come, ye rains, then, if ye will,
May's at home and with me still;
But come rather, thou good weather,
And find us in the fields together.
LEIGH HUNT.

LOVE'S PHILOSOPHY.

THE fountains mingle with the river,
　　And the rivers with the ocean;
The winds of heaven mix for ever,
　　With a sweet emotion;
Nothing in the world is single;
　　All things by a law divine
In one another's being mingle—
　　Why not I with thine?

See the mountains kiss high heaven,
　　And the waves clasp one another;
No sister flower would be forgiven
　　If it disdained its brother;
And the sunlight clasps the earth,
　　And the moonbeams kiss the sea;—
What are all these kisses worth,
　　If thou kiss not me?
PERCY BYSSHE SHELLEY.

MY LOVE.

I.

NOT as all other women are
Is she that to my soul is dear;
Her glorious fancies come from far,
Beneath the silver evening-star;
And yet her heart is ever near.

MAY.

II.

Great feelings hath she of her own,
Which lesser souls may never know;
God giveth them to her alone,
And sweet they are as any tone
Wherewith the wind may choose to blow.

III.

Yet in herself she dwelleth not,
Although no home were half so fair;
No simplest duty is forgot;
Life hath no dim and lowly spot
That doth not in her sunshine share.

IV.

She doeth little kindnesses,
Which most leave undone, or despise:
For naught that sets one heart at ease,
And giveth happiness or peace,
Is low-esteemed in her eyes.

V.

She hath no scorn of common things;
And, though she seem of other birth,
Round us her heart entwines and clings,
And patiently she folds her wings
To tread the humble paths of earth.

VI.

Blessing she is; God made her so;
And deeds of week-day holiness
Fall from her noiseless as the snow;
Nor hath she ever chanced to know
That aught were easier than to bless.

VII.

She is most fair, and thereunto
Her life doth rightly harmonize;
Feeling or thought that was not true
Ne'er made less beautiful the blue
Unclouded heaven of her eyes.

VIII.

She is a woman—one in whom
The spring-time of her childish years
Hath never lost its fresh perfume,

Though knowing well that life hath room
For many blights and many tears.

IX.

I love her with a love as still
As a broad river's peaceful might,
Which, by high tower and lowly mill,
Goes wandering at its own will,
And yet doth ever flow aright.

X.

And, on its full, deep breast serene,
Like quiet isles my duties lie;
It flows around them and between,
And makes them fresh and fair and green
Sweet homes wherein to live and die.

JAMES RUSSELL LOWELL.

COME INTO THE GARDEN, MAUD.

COME into the garden, Maud—
For the black bat, night, has flown!
Come into the garden, Maud,
I am here at the gate alone;
And the woodbine spices are wafted abroad,
And the musk of the roses blown.

For a breeze of morning moves,
And the planet of love is on high,
Beginning to faint in the light that she loves,
On a bed of daffodil sky,
To faint in the light of the sun that she loves,
To faint in its light, and to die.

All night have the roses heard
The flute, violin, bassoon;
All night has the casement jessamine stirred
To the dancers dancing in tune—
Till a silence fell with the waking bird,
And a hush with the setting moon,

I said to the lily, "There is but one
With whom she has heart to be gay.
When will the dancers leave her alone?
She is weary of dance and play."
Now half to the setting moon are gone,
And half to the rising day;

Low on the sand and loud on the stone
The last wheel echoes away.

I said to the rose, "The brief night goes
In babble and revel and wine.
O young lord-lover, what sighs are those,
For one that will never be thine!
But mine, but mine," so I sware to the rose,
. "For ever and ever, mine!"

And the soul of the rose went into my blood,
As the music clashed in the hall;
And long by the garden lake I stood,
For I heard your rivulet fall
From the lake to the meadow and on to
the wood—
O'er wood, that is dearer than all—

From the meadow your walks have left so
sweet
That whenever a March-wind sighs,
He sets the jewel print of your feet
In violets blue as your eyes—
To the woody hollows in which we meet,
And the valleys of Paradise.

The slender accacia would not shake
One long milk-bloom on the tree;
The white lake-blossom fell into the lake,
As the pimpernel dozed on the lea;
But the rose was awake all night for your
sake,
Knowing your promise to me;
The lilies and roses were all awake—
They sighed for the dawn and thee.

Queen rose of the rosebud garden of girls,
Come hither! the dances are done;
In gloss of satin and glimmer of pearls,
Queen lily and rose in one;
Shine out, little head, sunning over with
curls,
To the flowers, and be their sun.

There has fallen a splendid tear
From the passion-flower at the gate.
She is coming, my dove, my dear,
She is coming, my life, my fate!
The red rose cries, "She is near, she is
near;"

And the white rose weeps, "She is late;"
The larkspur listens, "I hear, I hear,"
And the lily whispers, "I wait."

She is coming, my own, my sweet!
Were it ever so airy a tread,
My heart would hear her and beat,
Were it earth in an earthly bed;
My dust would hear her and beat,
Had I lain for a century dead—
Would start and tremble under her feet,
And blossom in purple and red.
ALFRED TENNYSON.

THE SHIPWRECK.

IN vain the cords and axes were prepared,
For now the audacious seas insult the yard:
High o'er the ship they throw a horrid
shade,
And o'er her burst in terrible cascade.
Uplifted on the surge, to heaven she flies,
Her shattered top half buried in the skies,
Then headlong plunging, thunders on the
ground;
Earth groans! air trembles! and the deeps
 • resound!
Her giant bulk the dread concussion feels,
And quivering with the wound in torment
reels.
So reels, convulsed with agonizing throes,
The bleeding bull beneath the murderer's
blows.
Again she plunges! hark! a second shock
Tears her strong bottom on the marble
rock:
Down on the vale of death, with dismal
cries,
The fated victims, shuddering, roll their
eyes
In wild despair: while yet another stroke,
With deep convulsions, rends the solid oak:
Till like the mine, in whose infernal cell
The lurking demons of destruction dwell,
At length asunder torn her frame divides,
And, crashing, spreads in ruin o'er the tides.
O, were it mine with tuneful Maro's art
To wake to sympathy the feeling heart;

SHIPWRECK.

Like him the smooth and mournful verse
to dress
In all the pomp of exquisite distress,
Then too severely taught by cruel fate,
To share in all the perils I relate,
Then might I, with unrivalled strains de-
plore
The impervious horrors of a leeward shore!
  As o'er the surge the stooping mainmast
hung,
Still on the rigging thirty seamen clung;
Some, struggling, on a broken crag were
cast,
And there by oozy tangles grappled fast,
Awhile they bore the o'erwhelming bil-
lows' rage,
Unequal combat with their fate to wage;
Till, all benumbed and feeble, they forego
Their slippery hold, and sink to shades
below,
Some, from the main, yard-arm impetuous
thrown
On marble ridges, die without a groan.
Three with Palemon on their skill depend,
And from the wreck on oars and rafts de-
scend.
Now on the mountain wave on high they
ride,
Then downward plunge beneath the in-
volving tide,
Till one, who seems in agony to strive,
The whirling breakers heave on shore
alive;
The rest a speedier end of anguish knew,
And pressed the stony beach, a lifeless crew!

WILLIAM FALCONER.

WIDOW MACHREE.

I.

WIDOW machree, it's no wonder you frown—
  Och hone! widow machree
Faith, it ruins your looks, that same dirty
    black gown—
  Och hone! widow machree.

How altered your air,
With that close cap you wear—
'T is destroying your hair,
  Which should be flowing free:
Be no longer a churl
Of its black silken curl—
  Och hone! widow machree!

II.

Widow machree, now the summer is come—
  Och hone! widow machree
When every thing smiles, should a beauty
    look glum?
  Och hone! widow machree!
See the birds go in pairs,
And the rabbits and hares—
Why, even the bears
  Now in couples agree;
And the mute little fish,
Though they can 't spake, they wish—
  Och hone! widow machree.

III.

Widow machree, and when winter comes
    in—
  Och hone! widow machree—
To be poking the fire all alone is a sin,
  Och hone! widow machree.
Sure the shovel and tongs
To each other belongs,
And the kettle sings songs
  Full of family glee;
While alone with your cup,
Like a hermit you sup,
  Och hone! widow machree.

IV.

And how do you know, with the comforts
    I 've towld—
  Och hone! widow machree—
But you 're keeping some poor fellow out in
    the cowld,
  Och hone! widow machree!
With such sins on your head,
Sure your pence would be fled;
Could you sleep in your bed

Without thinking to see
Some ghost or some sprite,
That would wake you each night,
   Crying, " Och hone! widow ma-
    chree!"

v.

Then take my advice, darling widow ma-
    chree—
   Och hone! widow machree—
And with my advice, faith, I wish you 'd
    take me,
   Och hone! widow machree!
You 'd have me to desire
Then to stir up the fire;
   And sure hope is no liar
    In whispering to me,
That the ghosts would depart
When you 'd me near your heart—
   Och hone! widow machree!
            SAMUEL LOVER.

AFTER THE SEASON.

At last 't is over, doggie dear,
   The folks are fled, and town 's deserted:
The Park is desolate and drear,
   Where once we walked and—some girls
    —flirted.
Here, on the white cliff's grass-grown
    brink,
   'Neath which the blue sea frets and tosses,
We 'll rest ourselves awhile, and think
   About the season's gains and losses.

Ah me! It seems but yesterday
   The boughs with blossoms rich were
    laden;
It was the merry month of May,
   And I, a merry-hearted maiden.
Now, like a wild bird safely caged,
   A captor my lost heart is caging;—
What wonder I should be engaged
   To Guy, whose ways are so engaging?

Aunt Mary says that love 's a myth,
   And other heresies advances;
She vows she has no patience with
   A girl who throws away her chances.

My cousin hopes that " Eva knows
   What 's best, but must take leave to doubt
    it,"
And shakes her head—which only shows
   How little *she* can know about it!

It may not be in others' eyes
   A wealthy match; but I 've a notion
A wealth we never should despise
   Is that of firm and deep devotion.
And, as I say, when cousin Nell
   Laments that we can't keep a carriage,
Sometimes when young girls " marry well,"
   It doesn't prove a well-made marriage.

The Earl who filled my school-day dream
   When I was small and rather silly,
Might have supplied a splendid team
   To dash me down through Piccadilly.
But of this truth right sure am I:
   No mode of travel known at present
Compares to rambling on with Guy
   Thro' fields of fancy, fresh and pleasant!

The Earl would have grand castles, plac'd
   In several counties, I conjecture;
Arranged with most luxurious taste,
   Of most imposing architecture.
But where is one so rich and rare
   (Though practical old folks may quiz it)
As that grand castle in the air
   Which Guy and I so often visit?

Which are most precious, pure and bright,
   (I know how *I* should make selection!)
The gems that gleam with radiant light,
   Or eyes that beam with fond affection?
And Guy's so good, and true, and bold,
   With such a splendid air about him;
He should have been a knight of old—
   Only I could n't live without him!

I 'm sure 't is wise to marry Guy,
   For true love is a peerless blessing;
The way some parents let men buy
   Their daughters, is, I think, distressing.
I place that foremost 'mid the lot
   Of things that should at once be seen to;
I 'm sure it 's wise—and if it 's not,
   It does n't matter, for I mean to!
            ALFRED E. T. WATSON.

AFTER THE SEASON.

JENNY KISSED ME!

JENNY kissed me when we met,
  Jumping from the chair she sat in,
Time, you thief! who love to get
  Sweets into your list, put that in.
Say I 'm weary, say I 'm sad;
  Say.that health and wealth have missed
  me;
  Say I 'm growing old, but add—
        Jenny kissed me!
              LEIGH HUNT.

EXCUSE.

I TOO have suffered. Yet I know
She is not cold, though she seems so;
She is not cold, she is not light;
But our ignoble souls lack might.

She smiles and smiles, and will not sigh,
While we for hopeless passion die;
Yet she could love, those eyes declare,
Were but men nobler than they are.

Eagerly once her gracious ken
Was turned upon the sons of men;
But light the serious visage grew—
She looked, and smiled, and saw them
    through.

Our petty souls, our strutting wits,
Our labored puny passion-fits—
Ah, may she scorn them still, till we
Scorn them as bitterly as she!

Yet oh, that fate would let her see
One of some worthier race than we—
One for whose sake she once might prove
How deeply she who scorns can love.

His eyes be like the starry lights—
His voice like sounds of summer nights—
In all his lovely mien let pierce
The magic of the universe!

And she to him will reach her hand,
And gazing in his eyes will stand,
And know her friend, and weep for glee,
And cry—Long, long I 've looked for thee!

Then will she weep—with smiles, till then
Coldly she mocks the sons of men.
Till then her lovely eyes maintain
Their gay, unwavering, deep disdain.
              MATTHEW ARNOLD.

THE LANDING OF THE PILGRIM FATHERS IN NEW-ENGLAND.

" Look now abroad—another race has filled
  Those populous borders—wide the wood recedes,
  And towns shoot up, and fertile realms are tilled;
  The land is full of harvests and green meads."
              BRYANT.

THE breaking waves dashed high,
  On a stern and rock-bound coast,
And the woods against a stormy sky
  Their giant branches tossed;

And the heavy night hung dark,
  The hills and waters o'er,
When a band of exiles moored their bark
  On the wild New-England shore.

Not as the conqueror comes,
  They, the true-hearted, came;
Not with the roll of the stirring drums,
  And the trumpet that sings of fame;

Not as the flying come,
  In silence and in fear;—
They shook the depths of the desert gloom
  With their hymns of lofty cheer.

Amidst the storm they sang,
  And the stars heard, and the sea;
And the sounding aisles of the dim woods
    rang
  To the anthem of the free.

The ocean eagle soared
  From his nest by the white wave's foam;
And the rocking pines of the forest roared—
  This was their welcome home.

There were men with hoary hair
  Amidst that pilgrim band:
Why had they come to wither there,
  Away from their childhood's land?

There was woman's fearless eye,
  Lit by her deep love's truth;
There was manhood's brow serenely high
  And the fiery heart of youth.

What sought they thus afar?
  Bright jewels of the mine?
The wealth of seas, the spoils of war?—
  They sought a faith's pure shrine!

Ay, call it holy ground,
  The soil where first they trod;—
They have left unstained what there they
    found—
  Freedom to worship God.

                    FELICIA HEMANS.

THE BROOKLET.

SWEET brooklet, ever gliding,
  Now high the mountains riding,
The lone vale now dividing,
            Whither away?—
" With pilgrim course I flow,
  Or in summer's scorching glow,
Or o'er moonless wastes of snow,
            Nor stoop, nor stay:
For O, by high behest,
  To a bright abode of rest
In my parent Ocean's breast,
            I hasten away!"

Many a dark morass,
Many a craggy mass,
Thy feeble force must pass;
            Yet, yet delay!—

" Though the marsh be dire and deep,
Though the crag be stern and steep,
On, on my course must sweep;
            I may not stay:
For O, be it east or west,
To a home of glorious rest
In a bright sea's boundless breast,
            I hasten away!"

The warbling bowers beside thee
The laughing flowers that hide thee
With soft accord they chide thee,—
            Sweet brooklet, stay!
" I taste of the fragrant flowers,
I respond to the warbling bowers,
And sweetly they charm the hours
            Of my winding way;
But ceaseless still in quest
Of that everlasting rest
In my parent's boundless breast,
            I hasten away!"

Knowest thou that dread abyss?
Is it a scene of bliss?
O, rather cling to this,—
            Sweet brooklet, stay!
" O, who shall fitly tell
What wonders there may dwell?
That world of mystery well
            May strike dismay:
But I know 't is my parent's breast:
There held I must needs be blest,
And with joy to that promised rest
            I hasten away!"

                    SIR ROBERT GRANT.

THE CHARGE OF THE LIGHT
BRIGADE AT BALAKLAVA.

HALF a league, half a league,
  Half a league onward,
All in the valley of death,
  Rode the six hundred.

Into the valley of death
  Rode the six hundred;

THE BROOKLET.

For up came an order which
  Some one had blundered.
" Forward, the light brigade!
Take the guns!" Nolan said:
Into the valley of death,
  Rode the six hundred.

"Forward the light brigade!"
No man was there dismayed—
Not though the soldier knew
  Some one had blundered:
Theirs not to make reply,
Theirs not to reason why,
Theirs but to do and die—
Into the valley of death,
  Rode the six hundred.

Cannon to right of them,
Cannon to left of them,
Cannon in front of them,
  Volleyed and thundered.
Stormed at with shot and shell,
Boldly they rode and well;
Into the jaws of death,
Into the mouth of hell,
  Rode the six hundred.

Flashed all their sabres bare,
Flashed all at once in air,
Sabring the gunners there,
Charging an army, while
  All the world wondered.
Plunged in the battery smoke,
With many a desp'rate stroke
The Russian line they broke;
Then they rode back, but not—
  Not the six hundred.

Cannon to right of them,
Cannon to left of them,
Cannon behind them,
  Volleyed and thundered.
Stormed at with shot and shell,
While horse and hero fell,
Those that had fought so well
Came from the jaws of death,
Back from the mouth of hell,
All that was left of them,
  Left of six hundred.

When can their glory fade?
Oh the wild charge they made!
  All the world wondered.
Honor the charge they made!
Honor the light brigade,
  Noble six hundred!

ALFRED TENNYSON.

LAMENT OF THE IRISH EMI GRANT.

I 'm sittin' on the stile, Mary,
  Where we sat side by side
On a bright May mornin' long ago,
  When first you were my bride;
The corn was springin' fresh and green,
  And the lark sang loud and high;
And the red was on your lip, Mary,
  And the love-light in your eye.

The place is little changed, Mary;
  The day is bright as then;
The lark's loud song is in my ear,
  And the corn is green again;
But I miss the soft clasp of your hand,
  And your breath, warm on my cheek;
And I still keep list'nin' for the words
  You never more will speak.

'T is but a step down yonder lane,
  And the little church stands near—
The church where we were wed, Mary;
  I see the spire from here.
But the grave-yard lies between, Mary,
  And my step might break your rest—
For I 've laid you, darling, down to sleep,
  With your baby on your breast.

I 'm very lonely now, Mary—
  For the poor make no new friends;
But, oh! they love the better still
  The few our Father sends!
And you were all I had, Mary—
  My blessin' and my pride:
There 's nothing left to care for now,
  Since my poor Mary died.

Yours was the good, brave heart, Mary,
  That still kept hoping on,
When the trust in God had left my soul,
  And my arm's young strength was gone:
There was comfort ever on your lip,
  And the kind look on your brow—
I bless you, Mary, for that same,
  Though you cannot hear me now.

I thank you for the patient smile
  When your heart was fit to break—
When the hunger pain was gnawin' there,
  And you hid it for my sake;
I bless you for the pleasant word,
  When your heart was sad and sore—
Oh! I 'm thankful you are gone, Mary,
  Where grief can 't reach you more!

I 'm biddin' you a long farewell,
  My Mary—kind and true!
But I 'll not forget you, darling,
  In the land I 'm goin' to;
They say there 's bread and work for all,
  And the sun shines always there—
But I 'll not forget old Ireland,
  Were it fifty times as fair!

And often in those grand old woods
  I 'll sit, and shut my eyes,
And my heart will travel back again
  To the place where Mary lies;
And I 'll think I see the little stile
  Where we sat side by side,
And the springin' corn, and the bright May
    morn,
  When first you were my bride.

                              LADY DUFFERIN.

PLAYING WITH LOVE.

AGAIN the trees stand bare upon the moor,
  And bend their withered heads before the
    wind;
Again the snow is heaped up at the door,
  And frost is making many a fairy blind.
The spring sank into the summer-time, and
    June

Fell into autumn and her fruitful store;
December comes again to the old tune,
  And we are lovers still—and nothing
    more.

Now, why should we delay our own delight,
  Defer the hope, and wait for evil days
To cover love's young blossom with a
    blight,
  And sow the seeds of sorrow on our ways?
If we indeed have love enough to live,
  Why should we make a fear that is not
    now?
Or why should Fortune any blessing give,
  While we care not to woo her with a vow?

There is a time when life is life indeed,
  When love is love and all about it bright;
It is betrothal when great joy has need
  Of sleep to cool the hot heart of delight:
Because of you this sweetness came to me,
  And with a chain of flowers my life was
    led,
But after all what may the meaning be?
  Why, a betrothal if we may not wed.

Look at this picture, love; do you not see
  The sun flush on the summer's youngest
    bloom?
Here are three sisters; one of them will be
  A wife, and two will make their own
    dark doom:
See how they play with Love; but he will
    bring
A bitter day when they shall both atone,
And find too late the knowledge and its sting,
  That maids who play with Love may
    play alone.

Why will you give me but a little love,
  And spread it over many droning days?
Why for a little fault will you reprove,
  And spoil the harmony of pleasant ways?
If you will serve me so, then let the eyes
  Of my own fault accuse me while I live;
But I may learn it was not all a prize
  To win a woman who could not forgive.

PLAYING WITH LOVE.

It may be that you will not speak again,
But I have felt that I must come to say
That you have filled my weary weeks with
pain,
And I have had no peace for many a day:
Though you still hold the power that
would bless
My years, and with full joy my life
endow,
Yet your unkindness brings me to confess,
I never loved you less than I love now.

     *   *   *   *   *

Now in my heart of hearts I do rejoice,
And still I do repent for my hard speech,
Which turns upon me now that your dear
voice
Has placed the golden fruit within my
reach:
Let us be married in the early spring,
When blossoms bring new honey for the
bees,
And when new daisies come and new birds
sing,
And new green leaves come out upon
old trees.

                 —GUY ROSLYN.

FAITHLESS NELLY GRAY.

A PATHETIC BALLAD.

BEN BATTLE was a soldier bold,
And used to war's alarms;
But a cannon-ball took off his legs,
So he laid down his arms.

Now as they bore him off the field,
Said he, "Let others shoot:
For here I leave my second leg,
And the Forty-second foot."

The army-surgeons made him limbs:
Said he, "The 're only pegs:
But there 's as wooden members quite,
As represent my legs."

   ♦6

Now Ben he loved a pretty maid—
Her name was Nelly Gray;
So he went to pay her his devours,
When he devoured his pay.

But when he called on Nelly Gray,
She made him quite a scoff;
And when she saw his wooden legs.
Began to take them off.

"O, Nelly Gray! O, Nelly Gray!
Is this your love so warm?
The love that loves a scarlet coat
Should be more uniform."

Said she, "I loved a soldier once,
For he was blithe and brave;
But I will never have a man
With both legs in the grave.

"Before you had those timber toes
Your love I did allow;
But then, you know, you stand upon
Another footing now."

"O, Nelly Gray! O, Nelly Gray;
For all your jeering speeches,
At duty's call I left my legs
In Badajos's breaches."

"Why then," said she, "you 've lost the
feet
Of legs in war's alarms,
And now you cannot wear your shoes
Upon your feats of arms."

"O, false and fickle Nelly Gray!
I know why you refuse:
Though I 've no feet, some other man
Is standing in my shoes.

"I wish I ne'er had seen your face;
But, now, a long farewell!
For you will be my death;—alas!
You will not be my Nell!"

Now when he went from Nelly Gray
His heart so heavy got,
And life was such a burden grown,
It made him take a knot.

So round his melancholy neck
  A rope he did entwine,
And, for his second time in life,
  Enlisted in the line.

One end he tied around a beam,
  And then removed his pegs;
And, as his legs were off,—of course
  He soon was off his legs.

And there he hung, till he was dead
  As any nail in town;
For, though distress had cut him up,
  It could not cut him down.

A dozen men sat on his corpse,
  To find out why he died—
And they buried Ben in four cross-roads,
  With a stake in his inside.

                        THOMAS HOOD.

———

THE WELCOME.

COME in the evening, or come in the morn-
  ing;
Come when you're looked for, or come
  without warning;
Kisses and welcome you 'll find here before
  you,
And the oftener you come here the more
  I 'll adore you!
Light is my heart since the day we were
  plighted;
Red is my cheek that they told me was
  blighted;
The green of the trees looks far greener
  than ever,
And the linnets are singing, " True lovers
  don 't sever!"

I 'll pull you sweet flowers to wear if you
  choose them,
Or, after you 've kissed them, they 'll lie on
  my bosom;
I 'll fetch from the mountain its breeze to
  inspire you;
I 'll fetch from my fancy a tale that won't
  tire you.
Oh! your step's like the rain to the sum-
  mer-vexed farmer,

Or sabre and shield to a knight without
  armor;
I 'll sing you sweet songs till the stars rise
  above me,
Then, wandering, I 'll wish you in silence
  to love me.

We 'll look through the trees at the cliff
  and the eyrie;
We 'll tread round the rath on the track of
  the fairy;
We 'll look on the stars and we 'll list to the
  river,
Till you ask of your darling what gift you
  can give her.
Oh! she 'll whisper you,—" Love as un-
  changeably beaming,
And trust, when in secret most tunefully
  streaming
Till the starlight of heaven above us shall
  quiver,
As our souls flow in one down eternity's
  river."

So come in the evening, or come in the
  morning;
Come when you're looked for, or come
  without warning;
Kisses and welcome you 'll find here before
  you,
And the oftener you come the more I 'll
  adore you!
Light is my heart since the day we were
  · plighted;
Red is my cheek that they told me was
  blighted;
The green of the trees looks far greener
  than ever,
And the linnets are singing, " True lovers
  do n't sever!"

                        THOMAS DAVIS.

———

A FAREWELL TO TOBACCO.

May the Babylonish curse
Strait confound my stammering verse,
If I can a passage see
In this word-perplexity,
Or a fit expression find,
Or a language to my mind

THE WELCOME.

(Still the phrase is wide or scant),
To take leave of thee, great plant!
Or in any terms relate
Half my love, or half my hate;
For I hate, yet love, thee so,
That, whichever thing I shew,
The plain truth will seem to be
A constrained hyperbole,
And the passion to proceed
More for a mistress than a weed.

Sooty retainer to the vine!
Bacchus's black servant, negro fine!
Sorcerer! that mak'st us dote upon
Thy begrimed complexion,
And, for thy pernicious sake,
More and greater oaths to break
Than reclaimed lovers take
'Gainst women! Thou thy siege dost lay
Much, too, in the female way,
While thou suck'st the lab'ring breath
Faster than kisses, or than death.

Thou in such a cloud dost bind us
That our worst foes cannot find us,
And ill fortune, that would thwart us,
Shoots at rovers, shooting at us;
While each man, through thy height'ning
    steam,
Does like a smoking Etna seem;
And all about us does express
(Fancy and wit in richest dress)
A Sicilian fruitfulness.

Thou through such a mist dost show us
That our best friends do not know us,
And for those allowed features
Due to reasonable creatures,
Liken'st us to fell chimeras,
Monsters—that who see us, fear us;
Worse than Cerberus or Geryon,
Or, who first loved a cloud, Ixion.

Bacchus we know, and we allow
His tipsy rites. But what art thou,
That but by reflex can'st shew
What his deity can do—
As the false Egyptian spell
Aped the true Hebrew miracle?

Some few vapors thou may'st raise,
The weak brain may serve to amaze;
But to the reins and noble heart
Can'st nor life nor heat impart.

Brother of Bacchus, later born!
The old world was sure forlorn,
Wanting thee, tnat aidest more
The god's victories than, before,
All his panthers, and the brawls
Of his piping Bacchanals.
These, as stale, we disallow,
Or judge of thee meant: only thou
His true Indian conquest art;
And, for ivy round thy dart,
The reformed god now weaves
A finer thyrsus of thy leaves.

Scent to match thy rich perfume
Chemic art did ne'er presume—
Through her quaint alembic strain,
None so sovereign to the brain.
Nature, that did in thee excel,
Framed again no second smell.
Roses, violets, but toys
For the smaller sort of boys,
Or for greener damsels meant;
Thou art the only manly scent.

Stinkingest of the stinking kind!
Filth of the mouth and fog of the mind!
Africa, that brags her foyson,
Breeds no such prodigious poison!
Henbane, nightshade, both together,
Hemlock, aconite —— '

Nay, rather,
Plant divine, of rarest virtue!
Blisters on the tongue would hurt you!
'T was but in a sort I blamed thee;
None e'er prospered who defamed thee;
Irony all, and feigned abuse,
Such as perplext lovers use
At a need, when, in despair
To paint forth their fairest fair,
Or in part but to express
That exceeding comeliness
Which their fancies doth so strike,
They borrow language of dislike;

And, instead of dearest Miss,
Jewel, honey, sweetheart, bliss,
And those forms of old admiring,
Call her cockatrice and siren,
Basilisk, and all that 's evil,
Witch, hyena, mermaid, devil,
Ethiop, wench, and blackamoor,
Monkey, ape, and twenty more—
Friendly trait'ress, loving foe—
Not that she is truly so,
But no other way they know,
A contentment to express
Borders so upon excess
That they do not rightly wot
Whether it be from pain or not.

Or, as men, constrained to part
With what 's nearest to their heart,
While their sorrow 's at the height
Lose discrimination quite,
And their hasty wrath let fall,
To appease their frantic gall,
On the darling thing, whatever,
Whence they feel it death to sever,
Though it be, as they, perforce,
Guiltless of the sad divorce.

For I must (nor let it grieve thee,
Friendliest of plants, that I must) leave
    thee.
For thy sake, tobacco, I
Would do anything but die,
And but seek to extend my days
Long enough to sing thy praise.
But, as she, who once hath been
A king's consort, is a queen.
Ever after, nor will hate
Any tittle of her state
Though a widow, or divorced,
So I, from thy converse forced,
The old name and style retain,
A right Catherine of Spain;
And a seat, too, 'mongst the joys
Of the blest tobacco boys;
Where though I, by sour physician,
Am debarred the full fruition
Of thy favors, I may catch
Some collateral sweets, and snatch
Sidelong odors, that give life
Like glances from a neighbor's wife;

And still live in the by-places
And the suburbs of thy graces;
And in thy borders take delight,
An unconquered Canaanite.

Charles Lamb.

ONCE AND FOR AYE.

He sang as he lay on a Highland mountain,
    That English knight who had never
        known love,
" What song so sweet as the chiming
        fountain?
    What blue so blue as the heaven above?"
Fond heart!—for nearer and nearer drew
A sweeter voice and an eye more blue.

"O what can blush by the purple heather?
    What gold with the gorse-flower dare
        compare?"
He turned, fond heart, and found them to-
        gether
    On her glowing cheek and her glittering
        hair.
Now what for the knight are the hill
        flowers' dyes,
The fountain's voice and the sapphire skies?

She had lost her path, that Lowland lady,
    Whose heart had never a lord confessed;
O bright she blushed, and gentle prayed he
    Would guide her over the mountain crest.
And little loth was the gallant knight
To squire the steps of that lady bright.

So he took her hand, and they passed to-
        gether,
    The knight and the lady unlearned of
        love,
Through the golden gorse and the purple
        heather—
    O laughingly beamed the blue above.
And the fountain sang as their feet went
        by,
The Sibyl fountain—" *For aye—for aye.*"

The Author of "Songs of Killarney."

ONCE AND FOR AYE.

THE BATTLE OF LIMERICK.

YE genii of the nation,
Who look with veneration,
And Ireland's desolation onsaysingly de-
plore,
Ye sons of Gineral Jackson,
Who thrample on the Saxon,
Attend to the thransaction upon Shannon
shore.

When William, Duke of Schumbug,
A tyrant and a humbug,
With cannon and with thunder on our city
bore,
Our fortitude and valliance
Insthructed his battalions,
To rispict the galliant Irish upon Shannon
shore.

Since that capitulation,
No city in the nation
So grand a reputation could boast before,
As Limerick prodigious,
That stands with quays and bridges,
And ships up to the windies of the Shannon
shore.

A chief of ancient line,
'T is William Smith O'Brine,
Riprisints this darling Limerick this ten
years or more;
Oh the Saxons can 't endure
To see him on the flure,
And thrimble at the Cicero from Shannon
shore!

This valiant son of Mars
Had been to visit Par's,
That land of revolution, that grows the tri-
color;
And to welcome his return
From pilgrimages furren,
We invited him to tay on the Shannon
shore.

Then we summoned to our board
Young Meagher of the sword;

'T is he will sheathe that battle-axe in Saxon
gore;
And Mitchil of Belfast
We bade to our repast,
To dthrink a dish of coffee on the Shannon
shore.

Convaniently to hould
These patriots so bould,
We took the opportunity of Tim Doolan's
store;
And with ornamints and banners
(As becomes gintale good manners)
We made the loveliest tay-room upon Shan-
non shore.

'T would binifit your sowls
To see the butthered rowls,
The sugar-tongs and sangwidges and
craim gaylore,
And the muffins and the crumpets,
And the band of harps and thrumpets,
To celebrate the sworry upon Shannon
shore.

Sure the imperor of Bohay
Would be proud to dthrink the tay
That Misthress Biddy Rooney for O'Brine
did pour;
And, since the days of Strongbow,
There never was such Congo—
Mitchil dthrank six quarts of it—by Shan-
non shore.

But Clarndon and Corry
Connellan beheld this sworry
With rage and imulation in their black
heart's core;
And they hired a gang of ruffins
To interrupt the muffins,
And the fragrance of the Congo on the
Shannon shore.

When full of tay and cake,
O'Brine began to spake,
But juice a one could hear him, for a sud-
den roar
Of a ragamuffin rout
Began to yell and shout,
And frighten the propriety of Shannon
shore.

As Smith O'Brien harangued,
They batthered and they banged;
Tim Doolan's doors and windies down they
   tore;
They smashed the lovely windies
(Hung with muslin from the Indies),
Purshuing of their shindies upon Shannon
   shore.

With throwing of brickbats,
Drowned puppies and dead rats,
These ruffin democrats themselves did
   lower;
Tin kettles, rotten eggs,
Cabbage-stalks, and wooden legs,
They flung among the patriots of Shannon
   shore.

Oh, the girls began to scrame,
And upset the milk and crame;
And the honorable jintlemin they cursed
   and swore:
And Mitchil of Belfast,
'Twas he that looked aghast,
When they roasted him in effigy by Shan-
   non shore.

Oh, the lovely tay was spilt
On that day of Ireland's guilt;
Says Jack Mitchil, "I am kilt! Boys,
   where's the back door?
'Tis a national disgrace;
Let me go and veil me face!"
And he boulted with quick pace from the
   Shannon shore.

"Cut down the bloddy horde!"
Says Meagher of the sword,
"This conduct would disgrace any blacka-
   moor;"
But millions were arrayed,
So he shaythed his battle-blade,
Rethrayting undismayed from the Shannon
   shore.

Immortal Smith O'Brine
Was raging like a line;
'T would have done your sowl good to have
   heard him roar;

In his glory he arose,
And he rushed upon his foes,
But they hit him on the nose by the Shan-
   non shore.

Then the futt and the dthragoons
In squadthrons and platoons,
With their music playing chunes, down
   upon us bore;
And they bate the rattatoo,
And the Peelers came in view,
And ended the shaloo on the Shannon
   shore.

WILLIAM MAKEPEACE THACKERAY.

THE IVY-MAIDEN.

YOUR face, sweet Constance, and sur-
   roundings—
The ivy-wreath that rings you round—
Give full excuse for wild heart-boundings
And voice more tremulous in sound.
But Ivy's maidens "weep and ring,"
And you love best to laugh and tease;
Methinks some meaning marks the thing—
Ay, ivy means "intent to please."

But, dearest, at this fatal juncture,
I own, as empty is my purse
As bladder suffering from a puncture;
So, as for better or for worse
I can take no one—or, believe me,
I'd risk my chance of winning you—
Say, child, will you as friend receive me,
Your garland speaks of friendship true!

What! tears in those blue eyes indignant,
And quivering in those laughing lips?
Was then my proffer so malignant!
Ah, well, the blind boy often trips!
Suppose this New Year saw a twining
Of bridal wreaths for you and me,
I think 't would know of no repining:
Green ivy means "Fidelity."

THE IVY MAIDEN.

O sweet New Year! O sweet beginning
  Of strange new life to either soul!
O sudden start, triumphant winning,
  The start of life, and yet its goal!
Sweet Constance, with thine ivy-wreathing,
  Be to thine own surroundings true;
Nay, blush not at this whisper'd breathing
  That ivy tells of marriage too!

                    B. MONTGOMERIE RANKING.

MR. MOLONY'S ACCOUNT OF THE
BALL

GIVEN TO THE NEPAULESE AMBASSADOR BY THE PENINSULAR AND ORIENTAL COMPANY.

Oh will ye choose to hear the news?
  Bedad, I cannot pass it o'er:
I'll tell you all about the ball
  To the Naypaulase ambassador.
Begor! this fete all balls does bate
  At which I worn a pump, and I
Must here relate the splendthor great
  Of th' Oriental company.

These men of sinse dispoised expinse,
  To fete these black Achilleses.
"We'll show the blacks," says they, "Al-
    mack's,
  And take the rooms at Willis's."
With flags and shawls, for these Nepauls,
  They hung the rooms of Willis up,
And decked the walls, and stairs, and halls,
  With roses and with lilies up.
And Jullien's band it tuck its stand,
  So sweetly in the middle there,
And soft bassoons played heavenly chunes,
  And violins did fiddle there.
And when the coort was tired of spoort,
  I'd lave you, boys, to think there was
A nate buffet before them set,
  Where lashins of good dhrink there was!

At ten, before the ball-room door
  His moighty excellency was;
He smoiled and bowed to all the crowd—
  So gorgeous and immense he was.

His dusky shuit, sublime and mute,
  Into the dooway followed him;
And oh the noise of the blackguard boys,
  As they hurrood and hollowed him!

The noble chair stud at the stair,
  And bade the dthrums to thump; and he
Did thus evince to that black prince
  The welcome of his company.
Oh fair the girls, and rich the curls,
  And bright the oys you saw there was;
And fixed each oye, ye there could spoi,
  On Gineral Jung Bahawther was!

This gineral great then tuck his sate,
  With all the other ginerals,
(Bedad, his troat, his belt, his coat,
  All bleezed with precious minerals;)
And as he there, with princely air,
  Recloinin on his cushion was,
All round about his royal chair
  The squeezin and the pushin was.

O Pat, such girls, such jukes and earls,
  Such fashion and nobilitee!
Just think of Tim, and fancy him
  Amidst the hoigh gentility!
There was Lord De L'Huys, and the Porty-
    geese
  Ministher and his lady there;
And I reckonized, with much surprise,
  Our messmate, Bob O'Grady there.

There was Baroness Brunow, that looked
    like Juno,
  And Baroness Rehausen there,
And Countess Roullier, that looked pecu-
    liar
  Well in her robes of gauze, in there.
There was Lord Crowhurst (I knew him first
  When only Mr. Pips he was),
And Mick O'Toole, the great big fool,
  That after supper tipsy was.

There was Lord Fingall and his ladies all,
  And Lords Killeen and Dufferin,
And Paddy Fife, with his fat wife—
  I wondther how he could stuff her in,

There was Lord Belfast, that by me past,
  And seemed to ask how should *I* go there;
And the widow Macrae, and Lord A. Hay,
  And the marchioness of Sligo there.

Yes, jukes and earls, and diamonds and
    pearls,
  And pretty girls, was spooting there
And some beside (the rogues!) I spied
  Behind the windies, coorting there.
Oh, there's one I know, bedad would show
  As beautiful as any there;
And I'd like to hear the pipers blow,
  And shake a fut with Fanny there!
      WILLIAM MAKEPEACE THACKERAY.

THEY COME! THE MERRY SUMMER MONTHS.

THEY come! the merry summer months of
    beauty, song, and flowers;
They come! the gladsome months that
    bring thick leafiness to bowers.
Up, up, my heart! and walk abroad; fling
    cark and care aside;
Seek silent hills, or rest thyself where peace-
    ful waters glide;
Or, underneath the shadow vast of patriar-
    chal tree,
Scan through its leaves the cloudless sky
    in rapt tranquillity.

The grass is soft, its velvet touch is grateful
    to the hand;
And, like the kiss of maiden love, the breeze
    is sweet and bland;
The daisy and the buttercup are nodding
    courteously;
It stirs their blood with kindest love, to
    bless and welcome thee;
And mark how with thine own thin locks
    —they now are silvery gray—
That blissful breeze is wantoning, and
    whispering, "Be gay!"

There is no cloud that sails along the ocean
    of yon sky

But hath its own winged mariners to give
    it melody;
Thou seest their glittering fans outspread,
    all gleaming like red gold;
And hark! with shrill pipe musical, their
    merry course they hold.
God bless them all, those little ones, who'
    far above this earth,
Can make a scoff of its mean joys, and
    vent a noble mirth.

But soft! mine ear upcaught a sound,—
    from yonder wood it came!
The spirit of the dim green glade did
    breathe his own glad name;—
Yes, it is he! the hermit bird, that, apart
    from all his kind,
Slow spells his beads monotonous to the
    soft western wind;
Cuckoo! Cuckoo! he sings again,—his
    notes are void of art;
But simplest strains do soonest sound the
    deep founts of the heart.

Good Lord! it is a gracious boon for
    thought-crazed wight like me,
To smell again those summer flowers
    beneath this summer tree!
To suck once more in every breath their
    little souls away,
And feed my fancy with fond dreams of
    youth's bright summer day,
When, rushing forth, like untamed colt,
    the reckless truant boy
Wandered through green woods all day
    long, a mighty heart of joy!

I'm sadder now,—I have had cause; but
    O, I'm proud to think
That each pure joy-fount, loved of yore
    I yet delight to drink;—
Leaf, blossom, blade, hill, valley, stream,
    the calm, unclouded sky,
Still mingle music with my dreams, as in
    the days gone by
When summer's loveliness and light fall
    round me dark and cold,
I'll bear indeed life's heaviest curse—a
    heart that hath waxed old!
      WILLIAM MOTHERWELL.

H.W. Cutts Sr

THEY COME, THE MERRY SUMMER MONTHS.

THE PHANTOM.

AGAIN I sit within the mansion,
In the old, familiar seat;
And shade and sunshine chase each other
O'er the carpet at my feet.

But the sweet-brier's arms have wrestled
upwards
In the summers that are past,
And the willow trails its branches lower
Than when I saw them last.

They strive to shut the sunshine wholly
From out the haunted room—
To fill the house, that once was joyful,
With silence and with gloom

And many kind, remembered faces
Within the doorway come—
Voices, that wake the sweeter music
Of one that now is dumb.

They sing, in tones as glad as ever,
The songs she loved to hear;
They braid the rose in summer garlands,
Whose flowers to her were dear.

And still, her footsteps in the passage,
Her blushes at the door,
Her timid words of maiden welcome,
Come back to me once more.

And all forgetful of my sorrow,
Unmindful of my pain,
I think she has but newly left me,
And soon will come again.

She stays without, perchance, a moment,
To dress her dark-brown hair;
I hear the rustle of her garments—
Her light step on the stair!

O fluttering heart! control thy tumult,
Lest eyes profane should see
My cheeks betray the rush of rapture
Her coming brings to me!

She tarries long: but lo! a whisper
Beyond the open door—
And, gliding through the quiet sunshine,
A shadow on the floor!

Ah! 't is the whispering pine that calls me,
The vine whose shadow strays;
And my patient heart must still await her,
Nor chide her long delays.

But my heart grows sick with weary wait-
ing,
As many a time before:
Her foot is ever at the threshold,
Yet never passes o'er.

BAYARD TAYLOR.

A CANADIAN BOAT SONG.

Et remigem cantus hortatur.

QUINTILIAN.

FAINTLY as tolls the evening chime,
Our voices keep tune, and our oars keep
time.
Soon as the woods on shore look dim,
We 'll sing at St. Ann's our parting hymn.
Row, brothers, row! the stream runs fast,
The rapids are near and the daylight's past!

Why should we yet our sail unfurl:—
There is not a breath the blue wave to curl.
But when the wind blows off the shore
Oh! sweetly we 'll rest our weary oar.
Blow, breezes, blow! the stream runs fast,
The rapids are near, and the daylight's past!

Utawa's tide! this trembling moon
Shall see us afloat over thy surges soon.
Saint of this green isle, hear our prayers—
Oh! grant us cool heavens and favoring airs!
Blow, breezes, blow! the stream runs fast,
The rapids are near, and the daylight 's past!

THOMAS MOORE.

THE MINSTREL.

" WHAT voice, what harp, are those we hear
  Beyond the gate in chorus?
Go, page!—the lay delights our ear;
  We 'll have it sung before us!"
So speaks the king: the stripling flies—
He soon returns; his master cries—
  "Bring in the hoary minstrel!"

" Hail, princes mine! Hail, noble knights!
  All hail, enchanting dames!
What starry heaven! What blinding lights!
  Whose tongue may tell their names?
In this bright hall, amid this blaze,
Close, close, mine eyes! Ye may not gaze
  On such stupendous glories!"

The minnesinger closed his eyes;
  He struck his mighty lyre:
Then beauteous bosoms heaved with sighs,
  And warriors felt on fire;
The king, enraptured by the strain,
Commanded that a golden chain
  Be given the bard in guerdon.

" Not so! Reserve thy chain, thy gold,
  For those brave knights whose glances,
Fierce flashing through the battle bold,
  Might shiver sharpest lances!
Bestow it on thy treasurer there—
The golden burden let him bear
  With other glittering burdens.

" I sing as in the greenwood bush
  The cageless wild-bird carols—
The tones that from the full heart gush
  Themselves are gold and laurels!
Yet might I ask, then thus I ask—
Let one bright cup of wine, in flask
  Of glowing gold, be brought me!"

They set it down; he quaffs it all—
  "Oh! draught of richest flavor!
Oh! thrice divinely happy hall
  Where that is scarce a favor!
If heaven shall bless ye, think on me;
And thank your God as I thank ye
  For this delicious wine-cup!"

        JOHANN WOLFGANG VON GOETHE.
    Translation of JAMES CLARENCE MANGAN.

"YES!"

DEAR hiding-place, I pray you keep
  This secret in your breast;
O, fold it sure and fold it fast,
  And let it safely rest!
And let it rest and let it lie
  Till paling sky shall show
Through pearly pallor softly gray
  The flush of morning's glow.

For then—while dawn is still a dream,
  And all is hush'd and still—
Some one will cross the dewy fields
  That spread below the hill;
Will swiftly pass through flowering aisles,
  And crush the petals sweet—
Dear hiding-place, I pray you lay
  My secret at his feet!

Ah, cold and lifeless seems the word
  My trembling hand has traced;
He will not guess the thousand hopes
  That with that word are placed!
O, will he guess or will he know?
  Dear blossoms at my feet,
Look up and whisper faint and low:
  I long his eyes to meet.

Ah, happy letter, you will feel
  His touch so light and true!
Ah, happy hand that draws you forth,
  I would that I were you!
I would and would not—love and fear
  Make up so large a sum
Within my foolish heart to day,
  The heart that he has won.

O, have I lived or have I loved
  In any years before?
For now I cannot dream of joy,
  Save with him evermore.
I waste the days, the nights, the hours,
  In thoughts that come and go;
And yet in all their circling flight,
  One name alone they know.

O, lavish lights and floating shades,
  I would you were no more;
Fly down and haunt the midnight glades,
  And tell me day is o'er!

YES.

Dear ivy, keep my secret safe;
  Like him you cannot guess
That life and love are centered here
  Where I have written—" Yes!"

SONG.

STILL to be neat, still to be drest,
As you were going to a feast;
Still to be powdered, still perfumed—
Lady, it is to be presumed,
Though art's hid causes are not found;
All is not sweet, all is not sound.

Give me a look, give me a face,
That makes simplicity a grace;
Robes loosely flowing, hair as free—
Such sweet neglect more taketh me
Than all the adulteries of art;
They strike mine eyes, but not my heart.
                              BEN JONSON.

ABOU BEN ADHEM.

ABOU BEN ADHEM (may his tribe increase!)
Awoke one night from a deep dream of
    peace.
And saw within the moonlight in his room,
Making it rich, and like a lily in bloom,
An angel writing in a book of gold:
Exceeding peace had made Ben Adhem bold,
And to the presence in the room he said,
" What writest thou?"—The vision raised
    its head,
And, with a look made of all sweet accord,
Answered—" The names of those who love
    the Lord."
"And is mine one?" said Abou; "Nay,
    not so,"
Replied the angel.—Abou spoke more low,
But cheerly still; and said, " I pray thee,
    then,
Write me as one that loves his fellow-men."

The angel wrote, and vanished. The next
    night
It came again, with a great wakening light,
And showed the names whom love of God
    had blessed—
And, lo! Ben Adhem's name led all the
    rest!
                              LEIGH HUNT.

THE STEAMBOAT.

SEE how yon flaming herald treads
  The ridged and rolling waves,
As, crashing o'er their crested heads,
  She bows her surly slaves!
With foam before and fire behind,
  She rends the clinging sea,
That flies before the roaring wind,
  Beneath her hissing lee.

The morning spray, like sea-born flowers
  With heaped and glistening bells,
Falls round her fast in ringing showers,
  With every wave that swells;
And, flaming o'er the midnight deep,
  In lurid fringes thrown,
The living gems of ocean sweep
  Along her flashing zone.

With clashing wheel, and lifting keel,
  And smoking torch on high,
When winds are loud, and billows reel,
  She thunders, foaming, by!
When seas are silent and serene
  With even beam she glides,
The sunshine glimmering through the
    green
  That skirts her gleaming sides.

Now, like a wild nymph, far apart
  She views her shadowy form,
The beating of her restless heart
  Still sounding through the storm;
Now answers, like a courtly dame,
  The reddening surges o'er,
With flying scarf of spangled flame,
  The pharos of the shore.

To-night yon pilot shall not sleep,
  Who trims his narrowed sail;
To-night yon frigate scarce shall keep
  Her broad breast to the gale;
And many a foresail, scooped and strained,
  Shall break from yard and stay,
Before this smoky wreath hath stained
  The rising mist of day.

Hark! hark! I hear yon whistling shroud,
  I see yon quivering mast—
The black throat of the hunted cloud
  Is panting forth the blast!
An hour, and, whirled like winnowing chaff
  The giant surge shall fling
His tresses o'er yon pennon-staff,
  White as the sea-bird's wing!

Yet rest, ye wanderers of the deep!
  Nor wind nor wave shall tire
Those fleshless arms, whose pulses leap
  With floods of living fire;
Sleep on—and when the morning light
  Streams o'er the shining bay,
Oh, think of those for whom the night
  Shall never wake in day!

                OLIVER WENDELL HOLMES.

ABSENCE.

WHAT shall I do with all the days and
    hours
  That must be counted ere I see thy face?
How shall I charm the interval that lowers
  Between this time and that sweet time
    of grace?

Shall I in slumber steep each weary sense,—
  Weary with longing? shall I flee away
Into past days, and with some fond pretence
  Cheat myself to forget the present day?

Shall love for thee lay on my soul the sin
  Of casting from me God's great gift of
    time?
Shall I, these mists of memory locked
    within,
  Leave and forget life's purposes sublime?

O, how or by what means may I contrive
  To bring the hour that brings thee back
    more near?
How may I teach my drooping hope to live
  Until that blessed time, and thou art
    here?

I 'll tell thee; for thy sake I will lay hold
  Of all good aims, and consecrate to thee,
In worthy deeds each moment that is told
  While thou, beloved one! art far from me.

For thee I will arouse my thoughts to try
  All heavenward flights, all high and holy
    strains;
For thy dear sake, I will walk patiently
  Through these long hours, nor call their
    minutes pains.

I will this dreary blank of absence make
  A noble task-time, and will therein strive
To follow excellence, and to o'ertake
  More good than I have won since yet I
    live.

So may this doomed time build up in me
  A thousand graces, which shall thus be
    thine:
So may my love and longing hallowed be,
  And thy dear thought an influence di-
    vine.

                FRANCES ANNE KEMBLE.

THE VILLAGE BLACKSMITH.

UNDER a spreading chestnut tree
  The village smithy stands:
The smith—a mighty man is he,
  With large and sinewy hands;
And the muscles of his brawny arms
  Are strong as iron bands.

His hair is crisp, and black, and long;
  His face is like the tan,
His brow is wet with honest sweat—
  He earns whate'er he can;
And looks the whole world in the face,
  For he owes not any man.

ABSENCE.

Week in, week out, from morn till night,
　You can hear his bellows blow;
You can hear him swing his heavy sledge,
　With measured beat and slow—
Like a sexton ringing the village bell,
　When the evening sun is low.

And children, coming home from school,
　Look in at the open door;
They love to see the flaming forge,
　And hear the bellows roar,
And catch the burning sparks, that fly
　Like chaff from a threshing floor.

He goes on Sunday to the church,
　And sits among his boys;
He hears the parson pray and preach—
He hears his daughter's voice,
Singing in the village choir,
　And it makes his heart rejoice.

It sounds to him like her mother's voice,
　Singing in Paradise!
He needs must think of her once more,
　How in the grave she lies;
And with his hard, rough hand he wipes
　A tear out of his eyes.

Toiling, rejoicing, sorrowing—
　Onward through life he goes;
Each morning sees some task begin,
　Each evening sees it close—
Something attempted, something done,
　Has earned a night's repose.

Thanks, thanks to thee, my worthy friend,
　For the lesson thou has taught!
Thus at the flaming forge of life
　Our fortunes must be wrought—
Thus on its sounding anvil shaped
　Each burning deed and thought!

　　HENRY WADSWORTH LONGFELLOW.

VIRTUE.

SWEET day, so cool, so calm, so bright,
The bridal of the earth and sky!
The dew shall weep thy fall to-night;
　　For thou must die.

Sweet rose, whose hue, angry and brave,
Bids the rash gazer wipe his eye!
Thy root is ever in its grave—
　　And thou must die.

Sweet spring, full of sweet days and roses,
A box where sweets compacted lie!
Thy music shows ye have your closes,
　　And all must die.

Only a sweet and virtuous soul,
Like seasoned timber, never gives;
But, though the whole world turn to coal
　　Then chiefly lives.
　　　　GEORGE HERBERT.

SONG.

RARELY, rarely comest thou,
　Spirit of delight!
Wherefore hast thou left me now
　Many a day and night?
Many a weary night and day
'Tis since thou art fled away.

How shall ever one like me
　Win thee back again?
With the joyous and the free
　Thou wilt scoff at pain.
Spirit false! thou hast forgot
All but those who heed thee not.

As a lizard with the shade
　Of a trembling leaf,
Thou with sorrow art dismayed;
　Even the signs of grief
Reproach thee, that thou art near,
And reproach thou wilt not hear.

Let me set my mournful ditty
　To a merry measure:
Thou wilt never come for pity
　Thou wilt come for pleasure.
Pity then will cut away
　Those cruel wings, and thou wilt stay.

I love all that thou lovest,
　Spirit of delight!
The fresh earth in new leaves drest,

And the starry night;
Autumn evening, and the morn
When the golden mists are born.

I love snow, and all the forms
  Of the radiant frost;
I love waves and winds and streams,
  Everything almost
Which is nature's, and may be
Untainted by man's misery.

I love tranquil solitude,
  And such society
As is quiet, wise, and good;
  Between thee and me
What difference? but thou dost possess
The things I seek, not love them less.

I love love, though he has wings,
  And like light can flee,
But, above all other things,
  Spirit, I love thee:
Thou art love and life! oh, come,
Make once more my heart thy home!

       PERCY BYSSHE SHELLEY.

SAPPHO AND PHAON.

A LOVE-DUET.

Phaon sings at Sunset.

My lady, here I 'll linger,
  Conceal'd by clouds of night,
Until the morning's finger
  Shall touch the day with light.
When darkness round us closes,
  And silence strays with me,
The dew from garden roses
  Shall weep sad tears for thee.
The weary hours I 'll number
  When thou art lost to sight;
But song shall soothe thy slumber:
  My lady-love, good night!

Phaon sings at Dawn.

The lily-bells awaken,
  The rose no longer weeps,
The nests are all forsaken;
  But still my lady sleeps.
Glad daytime gives its blessing,
  And blossoms intertwine,
Thy window-ledge caressing
  With arms of eglantine.
But still the hours I number;
  I sorrow for thy sake:
Awaken from thy slumber,
  My lady-love, awake!

Phaon sings at Sunrise.

But hark! a footfall on the grass;
  It is her voice that greets the day.
Wake, blossoms, let your mistress pass;
  My lady comes—make way, make way!

Sappho sings at Sundown.

Farewell, glad sun, my heart is cold;
  Silence, ye birds, my love is dumb;
Sleep, flow'rets, whilst my arms enfold
  His shadow—for he will not come?

Farewell, farewell! see, I must die
  With fainting for the loss of thee.
Lost love! restore me with a sigh,
  And let thy kisses rain on me!

My Phaon, 't is our last farewell!
  Come back to me; I faint with pain!
When we are parted none will tell
  Thy heart to win me back again.

Farewell! and when the ocean wide
  Hath parted us, as it must part,
One sigh will draw me to thy side,
  One kiss will heal my broken heart.

       CLEMENT W. SCOTT.

ROBIN HOOD AND ALLEN-A-DALE.

COME listen to me, you gallants so free,
  All you that love mirth for to hear,
And I will tell you of a bold outlaw,
  That lived in Nottinghamshire.

SAPPHO AND PHAON.

As Robin Hood in the forest stood,
  All under the greenwood tree,
There he was aware of a brave young man,
  As fine as fine might be.

The youngster was clad in scarlet red,
  In scarlet fine and gay;
And he did frisk it over the plain,
  And chaunted a roundelay.

As Robin Hood next morning stood
  Amongst the leaves so gay,
There did he espy the same young man
  Come drooping along the way.

The scarlet he wore the day before
  It was clean cast away;
And at every step he fetched a sigh,
  "Alas! and a well-a-day!"

Then stepped forth brave Little John,
  And Midge, the miller's son;
Which made the young man bend his bow,
  When as he see them come.

"Stand off! stand off!" the young man said,
  "What is your will with me?"
"You must come before our master straight
  Under yon greenwood tree."

And when he came bold Robin before,
  Robin asked him courteously,
"O, hast thou any money to spare,
  For my merry men and me?"

"I have no money," the young man said,
  "But five shillings and a ring;
And that I have kept this seven long years,
  To have at my wedding.

"Yesterday I should have married a maid,
  But she was from me ta'en,
And chosen to be an old knight's delight,
  Whereby my poor heart is slain."

"What is thy name?" then said Robin
  Hood,
  "Come tell me, without any fail."
"By the faith of my body," then said the
  young man,
  "My name it is Allen-a-Dale."

"What wilt thou give me," said Robin
  Hood,
  "In ready gold or fee,
To help thee to thy true love again,
  And deliver her unto thee?"

"I have no money," then quoth the young
  man,
  "No ready gold nor fee,
But I will swear upon a book
  Thy true servant for to be."

"How many miles is it to thy true love?
  Come tell me without guile."
"By the faith of my body," then said the
  young man,
  "It is but five little mile."

Then Robin he hasted over the plain;
  He did neither stint nor lin,
Until he came unto the church
  Where Allen should keep his weddin'.

"What hast thou here?" the bishop then
  said,
  "I prithee now tell unto me,"
"I am a bold harper," quoth Robin Hood,
  "And the best in the north country."

"Oh welcome, oh welcome," the bishop
  he said;
  "That music best pleaseth me."
"You shall have no music," quoth Robin
  Hood,
  "Till the bride and the bridegroom I
  see."

With that came in a wealthy knight,
  Which was both grave and old;
And after him a finikin lass,
  Did shine like the glistering gold.

"This is not a fit match," quoth Robin
  Hood,
  "That you do seem to make here;
For since we are come into the church,
  The bride shall choose her own dear."

Then Robin Hood put his horn to his
 mouth,
And blew blasts two or three;
When four-and-twenty yeomen bold,
 Came leaping over the lea.

And when they came into the church-yard,
 Marching all in a row,
The first man was Allen-a-Dale,
 To give bold Robin his bow.

" This is thy true love," Robin he said,
 " Young Allen, as I hear say;
And you shall be married this same time,
 Before we depart away."

" That shall not be," the bishop he cried,
 " For thy word shall not stand;
They shall be three times asked into the
 church,
 As the law is of our land."

Robin Hood pulled off the bishop's coat,
 And put it upon Little John;
" By the faith of my body," the Robin said,
 " This cloth doth make thee a man."

When Little John went into the quire,
 The people began to laugh;
He asked them seven times into church,
 Lest three times should not be enough,

"Who gives me this maid?" said Little
 John,
Quoth Robin Hood, "That do I;
And he that takes her from Allen-a-Dale,
 Full dearly he shall her buy."

And then having ended this merry wedding,
 The bride looked like a queen;
And so they returned to the merry green-
 wood,
 Amongst the leaves so green.
     ANONYMOUS.

FAIRER THAN THEE.

FAIRER than thee, beloved,
 Fairer than thee;—
There is one thing, beloved,
 Fairer than thee.

Not the glad sun, beloved,
 Bright though it beams;
Not the green earth, beloved,
 Silver with streams;

Not the gay birds, beloved,
 Happy and free;
Yet there's one thing, beloved,
 Fairer than thee.

Not the clear day, beloved,
 Glowing with light;
Not (fairer still beloved)
 Star crowned night.

Truth, in her might, beloved,
 Grand in her sway;
Truth with her eyes, beloved,
 Clearer than day;

Holy and pure, beloved,
 Spotless and free,
Is the one thing, beloved,
 Fairer than thee.

Guard well thy soul, beloved,
 Truth dwelling there,
Shall shadow forth, beloved,
 Her image rare.

Then shall I deem, beloved,
 That thou art she;
And there'll be naught, beloved,
 Fairer than thee.
     ANONYMOUS.

A MATCH.

IF love were what the rose is,
 And I were like the leaf,
Our lives would grow together
In sad or singing weather,
Blown fields and flowerful closes,
 Green pleasure or grey grief;
If love were what the rose is,
 And I were like the leaf.

FAIRER THAN THEE.

If I were what the words are,
  And love were like the tune,
With double sound and single
Delight our lips would mingle,
With kisses glad as birds are
  That get sweet rain at noon;
If I were what the words are,
  And love were like the tune.

If you were life, my darling,
  And I, your love, were death,
We'd shine and snow together
Ere March made sweet the weather
With daffodil and starling
  And hours of fruitful breath;
If you were life, my darling,
  And I, your love, were death.

If you were thrall to sorrow,
  And I were page to joy,
We'd play for lives and seasons,
With loving looks and treasons,
And tears of night and morrow,
  And laughs of maid and boy;
If you were thrall to sorrow,
  And I were page to joy.

If you were April's lady,
  And I were lord in May,
We'd throw with leaves for hours,
And draw for days with flowers,
Till day like night were shady,
  And night were bright like day:
If you were April's lady,
  And I were lord in May.

If you were queen of pleasure,
  And I were king of pain,
We'd hunt down love together
Pluck out his flying-feather,
And teach his feet a measure,
  And find his mouth a rein;
If you were queen of pleasure,
  And I were king of pain.

ALGERNON CHARLES SWINBURNE.

AN AUTUMN IDYL.

Oh, knew he but his happiness, of men
The happiest he! who far from public rage,
Deep in the vale, with a choice few retired,
Drinks the pure pleasures of the rural life.
What though the dome be wanting, whose
    proud gate,
Each morning, vomits out the sneaking
    crowd,
Of flatterers false, and in their turn abused?
Vile intercourse! What though the glit-
    tering robe
Of every hue reflected light can give,
Or floating loose, or stiff with mazy gold,
The pride and gaze of fools! oppress him
    not?
What though, from utmost land and sea
    purvey'd,
From him each rarer tributary life
Bleeds not, and his insatiate table heaps
With luxury, and death? What though
    his bowl
Flames not with costly juice; nor sunk in
    beds,
Oft of gay care, he tosses out the night,
Or melts the thoughtless hours in idle state?
What though he knows not those fantastic
    joys,
That still amuse the wanton, still deceive;
A face of pleasure, but a heart of pain;
Their hollow moments undelighted all?
Sure peace is his; a solid life, estranged
To disappointment, and fallacious hope;
Rich in content, in Nature's bounty rich,
In herbs and fruits. Whatever greens the
    Spring,
When heaven descends in showers; or
    bends the bough
When Summer reddens, and when Autumn
    beams;
Or in the Wintry glebe whatever lies
Conceal'd, and fattens with the richest sap:
These are not wanting; nor the milky drove,
Luxuriant, spread o'er all the lowing vale;
Nor bleating mountains; nor the chide of
    streams,
And hum of bees, inviting sleep sincere
Into the guiltless breast, beneath the shade,

Or thrown at large amid the fragrant hay,
Nor aught besides of prospect, grove or
    song,
Dim grottoes, gleaming lakes and fountains
    clear.
Here too dwells simple Truth; plain Inno-
    cence;
Unsullied Beauty; sound unbroken Youth,
Patient of labor, with a little pleased;
Health ever blooming; unambitious Toil,
Calm Contemplation, and poetic Ease.

Let others brave the flood in quest of gain,
And beat, for joyless months, the gloomy
    wave:
Let such as deem it glory to destroy,
Rush into blood, the sack of cities seek,
Unpierced, exulting in the widow's wail,
The virgin's shriek, and infant's trembling
    cry:
Let some, far distant from their native soil,
Urged on by want or harden'd avarice,
Find other lands beneath another sun:
Let this through cities work his eager way,
By legal outrage and established guile,
The social-sense extinct; and that ferment
Mad into tumult the seditious herd,
Or melt them down to slavery: let these
Insnare the wretched in the toils of law,
Fomenting discord, and perplexing right,
An iron race! and those of fairer front,
But equal inhumanity, in courts,
Delusive pomp, and dark cabals, delight;
Wreathe the deep bow, diffuse the lying
    smile,
And tread the weary labyrinth of state: —
While he, from all the stormy passions free
That restless men involve, hears, and but
    hears,
At distance safe, the human tempest roar,
Wrapp'd close in conscious peace. The
    fall of kings,
The rage of nations, and the crush of states,
Move not the man who, from the world
    escaped,
In still retreats, and flowery solitudes,
To Nature's voice attends, from month to
    month
And day to day, through the revolving
    year:
Admiring, sees her in every shape;

Feels all her sweet emotions at his heart,
Takes what she liberal gives, nor thinks
    of more.
He, when young Spring protrudes the
    bursting gems,
Marks the first bud, and sucks the health-
    ful gale
Into his freshen'd soul. Her genial hours
He full enjoys; and not a beauty blows,
And not an opening blossom breathes in
    vain.
In summer, he beneath the living shade,
Such as o'er frigid Tempe wont to wave,
Or Hemus cool, reads what the Muse, of
    these,
Perhaps, has in immortal numbers sung;
Or what she dictates writes: and, oft an
    eye
Shot round, rejoices in the vigorous year.
When Autumn's yellow lustre gilds the
    world,
And tempts the sickled swain into the field,
Seized by the general joy, his heart distends
With gentle throes; and, through the tepid
    gleams
Deep musing, then he best exerts his song.
E'en Winter wild, to him is full of bliss.
The mighty tempest, and the hoary waste,
Abrupt and deep, stretch'd o'er the buried
    earth,
Awake to solemn thought. At night the
    skies
Disclosed, and kindled by refining frost,
Pour every lustre on th' exalted eye.
A friend, a book, the stealing hours secure,
And mark them down for wisdom. With
    swift wing,
O'er land and sea imagination roams;
Or truth, divinely breaking on his mind,
Elates his being, and unfolds his powers;
Or in his breast heroic virtue burns.
The touch of kindred too and love he feels;
The modest eye, whose beams on his alone
Ecstatic shine; the little strong embrace
Of prattling children, twined around his
    neck,
And emulous to please him, calling forth
The fond parental soul. Nor purpose gay,
Amusement, dance, or song, he sternly
    scorns;

AN AUTUMN IDYL.

For happiness and true philosophy
Are of the social, still, and smiling kind.
This is the life which those who fret in
guilt,
And guilty cities, never knew; the life,
Led by primeval ages, uncorrupt,
When Angels dwelt, and GOD himself
with man!

—JAMES THOMPSON.

AT A MODERN SHRINE.

WITH a spray of shower-wet lilac in your
hand,
There you stand;
And an April sun is glinting on your hair.
Are you not incarnate Spring?
Can I limn you? 'T were a thing
That might drive a defter artist to despair.

May not fancy hear Arcadian sheep-bells
tinkle,
As you sprinkle
Diamond droplets from that fragrant purple
spire?
Is the hyacinth's own hue
Of a sweeter, suaver blue
Than your eyes of soft and silken-shaded
fire?

Yet no unsubstantial allegoric thing,
Like the Spring
Of the poets and the painters, love, are you,
Not a sylph, but sweetly human,
And a very, very woman,
Though you look as though compact of
sun and dew.

And you will not, like a vision, melt in
air,
If I dare
To engirdle you with merely mortal arm:
Proudly blest to so environ
Such a super-dainty siren,
Unafraid of ghostly flight, or evil charm.

You're a merry mortal maiden, and no
myth,
Like Lilith,
Or the briny beauties shunned by sage
Ulysses;
Your drift of sunny hair
Is no silky-subtle snare,
And your lips were never shaped for cruel
kisses.

Yet you catch and keep my heart, and show
no mercy, Little Circe,
And in sooth I'm quite resigned to such a
capture.
Who'd resist or turn a railer
At so generous a gaoler?
Lo! I yield to love's restraint with ready
rapture.

Ay, your voice is very sweet and most
seductive,
Yet productive
Of no peril, and no sudden pang, and sharp.
Near your swift and sweeping finger,
'T is as safe as sweet to linger,
For you play on the piano—not the harp!

So! you shake a saucy head, and swear I
flatter!
Well, what matter?
I prefer you much to all the classic ladies,
Be they goddesses or graces,
And whatever be their places,
From the heaven kist Olympus down to—
Hades!

"There is nothing very classical about
you?"—
Well, I doubt you,
You've a soft Ionic air, a grace that's
Attic;
Yet I own you're not antique,
And for English over Greek,
I avow that I've a preference emphatic.

There is many a little trifler with the
Muses,
Who abuses
Everything that is post-Phidian and pretty;

But all loveliness is no man's
And the Grecians, and the Romans,
Did not turn out a Turner or an Etty.

I think that theirs was not the *only* Charis,
And that Paris
Might distribute a whole orchard, love,
to-day,
And yet appear invidious;
Praxiteles and Phidias
Shake hands with Leech and Leighton
and Millais.

I am sure your hair has hyacinthine grace,
And your face
Is as sweet and pure as any marble Clyte;
And, although you 're scarce at
home
In the clouds or on the foam,
You 're a perfect *terra firma* Aphrodite.

Did not Gibson perpetrate a tinted Venus?
(Which, between us,
Was a saucer-eyed and saffron-hued delu-
sion)
But I swear, my darling, that you
Are like poor Pygmalion's statue,
When just flushing with life's roseate suf-
fusion.

If you 're scarcely statuesque, you 're sweet
and simple,
And that dimple
That is lurking underneath your lower lip,
Is a charm the marble misses;
Oh! a fig for Parian kisses
While from such a rosy chalice I may sip.

Let Anacreon, let Horace and Tibullus,
Or Catullus,
Sing of Lalage and Pyrrha and the rest of
them,
I 'll back my British beauty,
From her chignon to her shoe-tie,
To compete in grace and sweetness with
the best of them.

Oh! you say my pretty talk is most mis-
leading—
Special pleading!

Now, that really is exceedingly ungracious.
I protest that my defence
Of the present's no pretence,
And my praise of your sweet self is most
veracious.

I 've a very great respect for Attic art,
For my part,
Yet I think, in spite of ultra-classic sages,
That the grand Hellenic story
Don 't exhaust creation's glory,
And that Nature's is a book of many pages.

I believe that, could I see a Grecian goddess
In a bodice
Poppy-hued, and skirts the color of the
wheat;
With a spray of lilac blossom
In her chastely-covered bosom,
I should find my British darling just as
sweet.

Love and loveliness can never be antique,
And the Greek
No monopoly of either I 'll allow;
And I really do not care
For the whole of Lempriere,
While to such a modern goddess I may
bow.

E. J. M.

FIDELITY.

A BARKING sound the shepherd hears,
A cry as of a dog or fox;
He halts,—and searches with his eyes
Among the scattered rocks:
And now at distance can discern
A stirring in a brake of fern;
And instantly a dog is seen,
Glancing through that covert green.

The dog is not of mountain breed;
Its motions, too, are wild and shy—
With something, as the shepherd thinks,
Unusual in its cry;
Nor is there any one in sight
All round, in hollow or on height;

AT A MODERN SHRINE.

Nor shout nor whistle strikes his ear.
What is the creature doing here?
It was a cove, a huge recess,
That keeps, till June, December's snow;
A lofty precipice in front,
A silent tarn below!
Far in the bosom of Helvellyn,
Remote from public road or dwelling,
Pathway, or cultivated land,—
From trace of human foot or hand.

There sometimes doth a leaping fish
Send through the tarn a lonely cheer;
The crags repeat the raven's croak
In symphony austere;
Thither the rainbow comes, the cloud,
And mists that spread the flying shroud;
And sunbeams; and the sounding blast,
That, if it could, would hurry past;
But that enormous barrier holds it fast.

Not free from boding thoughts, awhile,
The shepherd stood; then makes his way
O'er rocks and stones, following the dog
As quickly as he may;
Nor far had gone before he found
A human skeleton on the ground.
The appalled discoverer with a sigh
Looks round, to learn the history.

From those abrupt and perilous rocks
The man had fallen, that place of fear!
At length upon the shepherd's mind
It breaks, and all is clear.
He instantly recalled the name,
And who he was, and whence he came;
Remembered, too, the very day
On which the traveller passed this way.

But hear a wonder, for whose sake
This lamentable tale I tell!
A lasting monument of words
This wonder merits well.
The dog, which still was hovering nigh,
Repeating the same timid cry,
This dog had been through three months
     space
A dweller in that savage place.

Yes, proof was plain that, since that day
When this ill-fated traveller died,
The dog had watched about the spot,
Or by his master's side.
How nourished here through such long
     time
He knows who gave that love sublime,
And gave that strength of feeling, great
Above all human estimate!

WILLIAM WORDSWORTH.

THE HOLLY-TREE.

O READER! hast thou ever stood to see
     The holly-tree!
The eye that contemplates it well, perceives
     Its glossy leaves
Ordered by an intelligence so wise
As might confound the atheist's sophistries

Below, a circling fence, its leaves are seen
     Wrinkled and keen;
No grazing cattle, through their prickly
     round,
     Can reach to wound;
But as they grow where nothing is to fear,
Smooth and unarmed the pointless leaves
     appear.

I love to view these things with curious eye
     And moralize;
And in this wisdom of the holly-tree
     Can emblems see
Wherewith, perchance, to make a pleasant
     rhyme,
One which may profit in the after-time.

Thus, though abroad, perchance, I might
     appear
     Harsh and austere—
To those who on my leisure would intrude,
     Reserved and rude;
Gentle at home amid my friends I'd be,
Like the high leaves upon the holly-tree.

And should my youth, as youth is apt, I
know,
  Some harshness show,
All vain asperities I, day by day,
  Would wear away,
Till the smooth temper of my age should be
Like the high leaves upon the holly-tree.

And as, when all the summer trees are seen
  So bright and green,
The holly-leaves their fadeless hues display
  Less bright than they;
But when the bare and wintry woods we see,
What then so cheerful as the holly-tree?

So, serious should my youth appear among
  The thoughtless throng;
So would I seem, amid the young and gay,
  More grave than they;
That in my age as cheerful I might be
As the green winter of the holly-tree.

                    ROBERT SOUTHEY.

————

BY THE LILIES.

WHITE swans beside the lilies, the lilies
  golden-eyed,
The lilies white and foam tipp'd, in snowy
  dress of bride;
Their broad green leaflets floating upon the
  silver stream,
And, ah! the fairest lily drifting in a dream;

With paddles deftly balanced by her small
  fingers white,
Her light canoe slow moving, mid the
  rushes out of sight;
Her golden hair low floating adown the
  vest of blue,
Her sweet eyes on the river fill'd with tender dew.

If there *was* a time when elfies, when
  brownies, and when fays
Stole the heart from loving manhood, sure
  have come again those days;

One *may* dream it, one *must* feel it, when in
  balmy summer air,
One's heart away is stolen by sweet winsome girlhood fair.
                    —ANONYMOUS.

————

THE PAINTER'S WALK.

I.

IN THE WOOD.

(The Husband speaks.)

BETWEEN gray trunks the curving path-
  way runs,
  Now in, now out; gray trunks of ancient
    trees
Barred with soft shadow-bands, where falls
  the sun's
  Ray slantwise through the wood, and on
    the breeze
Rising and flutt'ring, rustling light,
The dry brown leaves make answer, as the
  sight
Of so much life renewed spoke hopefully—
A green youth yet for them which should
  not die!

Here is a space cleared by the woodman's
  arm.
  We two will rest awhile, and lying low
Under this beech tree, nigh a budding palm
  Thick set with silver bloom, note idly
    how
Each tree is redd'ning to the Spring,
Who soon a tender cloud of green will fling
Over these twigs, athwart this tracery
Of slender boughs seen black against the
  sky.

No noises from the town can vex us here,
  But softened by long distance comes the
    shrill
Sound of sharp plows; and, far away, the
  clear
  Soft whistle of a woodman; further still
Falls from an upland farm the bleat
Of new-born lambs; and mournful now,
  but sweet,

BY THE LILIES.

A ring-dove in a twisted thorn hard by
Tempers earth's joy with her sad monody.

Though gray the thorn is still, that soon
  will be
    White with soft bloom; though mute the
      nightingale;
Though not a primrose or anemone
    Has ventured to put forth a blossom pale;
Yet does this sight of white clouds fleet
Across the sky, and all those sounds that
  greet
Our eager souls thirsting for summer's
  tune,
Thrill us with promise of the coming June.

Now sing with your low fluted voice,
  while I
    Lie with closed eyes, and fancy all around
Are summer's dreamy songs, and greenery
    On these poor leafless trees, and all the
      ground
Purple with scented orchis flowers,
And the world young again, and all time
  ours
To do great works in—I, wise, great of fame,
And you—ah! you alone I'd keep the same.

———

(The Wife sings.)

The day breaks and the throstle sings,
The joyful lark has spread his wings;
The whole green world thrills to his tune,
And wakes to greet this day of June!
    Wake, love! rejoice!

Drops hang on every hedgerow leaf,
They shine like tears of happy grief.
The daisy cups are fringed with dew
As your eyes when I say "Adieu!"
    Oh! sing, sweet voice!

A new bud on your Provence rose,
Since last night's ling'ring through the
  close,
Hangs down a loosened woodbine trail
And for your window makes a veil!
    Dear eyes, shine through!

There sing upon the hawthorn bush
The bold blackbird and sweeter thrush.
The rolling clouds leave heaven blue,
The eager sun but waits for you!
    Waits, love, for you!

———

(The Husband speaks.)

Dear voice, cease not; even the round-eyed
  dove
    Is silent, listening to your sweeter note.
And I could listen ever, knowing love
    Is only grown, since first those words I
      wrote.
Grown, but not changed, unless it be
To take a nobler form; for now I see
How year by year my love has rooted been
In deeper ground than youth and beauties
  seen!

II.

IN THE MEADOW.

Here is an idle rhyme to make you smile,
    Or sigh, perhaps, if truth it seem to fold.
Sit here and read it, but believe the while,
    I love so well, to me you'll ne'er be old.

———

A painter to his wife one day:
    This sunset hour brings back to me,
I know not why, the radiant day,
    When first my love you vowed to be.

Go, then; put on that very gown,
    And hold these cowslips in your hand,
And let your hair flow rippling down,
    That once more I may see you stand.

A shy surprise in your blue eyes,
    And on your lips a dawning smile,
The smile at my wild words. Surprise
    That I could doubt your love a while.

Ah! so; just so! and yet—alas!
　Though sweeter since is grown your face,
Though dearer every day we pass,—
　I miss a bloom, a vanished grace.

Yes, vain it is in summer's prime
　To seek the buds of April's day.
For time is passing!......Ah! not Time!
　'T is *we*, my love, who pass away!

————

Sad words, but true! So says your face
　　grown grave,
　As slow your eyes have travelled o'er
　　the page.
Sad thoughts! which seem to mock this
　　sunshine brave.
　Such April morns, what's Time to us, or
　　Age?

Are we not happy, rich in hope and love,
　Having our youth together, and one
　　heart,
One mind and will between us, God above:
　His sunshine round about us; and fair
　　Art.

To serve with reverent hands? Look up
　　again,
　And chase the gravity from eyelids wet;
Let us be gay as yestermorn—for vain
　And idle is such fanciful regret!

————

III.

BY THE RIVER.

(The Wife speaks.)

Oh! to be idle one long day!
　When spring is almost over;
And these great giants gaunt and gray
　Are green; when roundhead clover

And purple thyme-tufts fill the air,
　And fields are gay with daisies;
When, blushing, dies the hawthorn fair
　Just as your Poet praises.

When overhead the lark's far song,
　And thrushes in the hedgerows,
And hidden linnets piping long
　Where rank the river sedge grows.

Oh! to be idle one spring day,
　To muse in wood or meadow;
Glide down this river 'twixt the play
　Of sun and trembling shadow!

I'd see all wonders 'neath the stream,
　The pebbles and vext grasses;
I'd lean across the boat and dream
　As each scene slowly passes.

The tide should ripple welcomes low
　And dance the kingcups bravely
And flags in purple stately bow
　And nod the tall reeds gravely.

I'd rest an hour the willows by
　And say a prayer in pity,
For all who stifle, groan and die,
　This day in crowded city.

IV.

SUNSET.

(The Wife speaks.)

Sitting once in the twilight
　I watched the fire-flare
Red glowing, and suddenly bright'ning
　Upon your face and hair.

It gave strange light and shadow,
　An unfamiliar look;
I had to learn you over again
　Bending over your book.

But when you broke the silence,
　And read those burning words
Great poets have spent themselves to write,
　My heart leapt up towards

And to your voice made answer,
　Which, like a wail of pain,

Or autumn winds in swaying trees
 Did rise and fall again,

And rise; inspired by passion—
 By passion, hope, or dread—
You seemed a poet then, and I
 Forgot you only read.

Then, turning o'er the pages,
 You read a song I knew;
'T was then the present vanished;
 There was nor I, nor you,

But a little child in a garden,
 Reading with puzzled air
An old hand-written volume,
 Finding those verses there.

For years 'tween tarnished covers
 That passion-song had lain:
The hand that wrote it slept beneath
 Two purple lilac's rain.

And as you read, I loitered
 Under the shade of trees,
And smelt the fragrant lavender
 Swayed by the humming bees.

Child-like, again I wondered
 What meant such sad, sore grief,
And why the dead hand wrote that song,
 Marking against the leaf

A cross, and a date forgotten,
 In pale and faded ink,—
I could almost feel the summer wind
 Fresh from the river brink!

You paused.. "Well, there 's the song, love!
 You like it?" Ah! then fled
My dreams. I answered: ".Forgive me, I
 Heard not a word you read!"

But that this bright eve's glory
 May live again some day,
Read me aloud some stirring story
 Or poet's sad, sweet lay.

    *   *   *   *   *

———

(The Husband speaks.)

There in that leaf we shut.it,
 An embalmed happiness!
Now homewards, wife. Has there been
 melody!
 To-day? True eyes, confess.
 —A. L. B.

———

MY HARVEST "EVE."

O FOR the glory of harvest time!
I sing it in song and sing it in rhyme.
With blush of the beauteous summer's
 prime
 On its dewy dawns,
 And its hazy morns,
And gathered grainage of golden corns.

O for the glory of harvest time!
I weave it in song and sing it in rhyme,
While happy hours their passage chime;
 And every breath
 So softly saith
"There 's life new born with the summer's
 death."

O for the glory of golden noon,
And purpled heather, and ripened bloom,
And full-orbed splendor of harvest moon—
 The dangerous moon,
 That fades so soon
From starry splendor to starless gloom!

    *   *   *   *   *

Oh for the peerless face that shines
Out from the lattice beyond the limes!
Harvest queen of my harvest time,
How shall I praise her in song or rhyme,
 With her tangled tresses
 And eyes divine?

I 'll set her amidst the ripened sheaves,
Or golden glory of burnished leaves:
Flowers and fruits in the autumn eves,
Fairest "Eve" of them all is she—
 My harvest queen
 From o'er the lea!

O for the lady of brow serene!
How shall I praise her, the manor queen,
With the ebon gloss on her ringlets sheen?
   Never a tangled tress is seen,
   Nor saucy eyes to dance and gleam.
   Like eyes that dazzle my rhymes, I
      ween.

O for a heart to shrine them both!
Either to lose or leave I 'm loth,
For love has grown with the harvest growth.
   O gathered grain,
   Know you this pain?
Can severed ties be blent again?

The grain is gathered, shadows fall
O'er land and lea like sombre pall;
My heart and I are still in thrall;
   Your eyes will shine
   Starlike to mine,
My Eve, for every harvest time?

                              —RITA.

———

A WOMAN'S QUESTION.

BEFORE I trust my fate to thee,
   Or place my hand in thine,
Before I let thy future give
   Color and form to mine,
Before I peril all for thee,
Question thy soul to-night for me.

I break all slighter bonds, nor feel
   A shadow of regret:
Is there one link within the past
   That holds thy spirit yet?
Or is thy faith as clear and free
As that which I can pledge to thee?

Does there within thy dimmest dreams
   A possible future shine,
Wherein thy life could henceforth breathe.
   Untouched, unshared by mine?
If so, at any pain or cost,
O, tell me before all is lost!

Look deeper still: if thou canst feel,
   Within thy inmost soul,
That thou hast kept a portion back,
   While I have staked the whole,
Let no false pity spare the blow,
But in true mercy tell me so.

Is there within thy heart a need
   That mine cannot fulfil?
One chord that any other hand
   Could better wake or still?
Speak now, lest at some future day
My whole life wither and decay. .

Lives there within thy nature hid
   The demon-spirit change,
Shedding a passing glory still
   On all things new and strange?
It may not be thy fault alone,—
But shield my heart against thy own.

Couldst thou withdraw thy hand one day
   And answer to my claim,
That fate, and that to-day's mistake,—
   Not thou,—had been to blame?
Some soothe their conscience thus; but thou
Wilt surely warm and save me now.

Nay, answer *not*,—I dare not hear,
   The words would come too late;
Yet I would spare thee all remorse,
   So comfort thee my fate:
Whatever on my heart may fall
Remember, I *would* risk it all!

             —ADELAIDE ANNE PROCTER.

———

SONNETS.

WHEN I do count the clock that tells the
      time.
And see the brave day sunk in hideous
      night;
When I behold the violets past prime,
And sable curls all silvered o'er with white:
When lofty trees I see barren of leaves,
Which erst from heat did canopy the herd,
And Summer's green all girded up in
      sheaves,

A WOMAN'S QUESTION.

·Borne on the bier with white and bristly
    beard;
Then, of thy beauty do I question make,
That thou among the wastes of time must
    go,
Since sweets and beauties do themselves
    forsake,
And die as fast as they see others grow;
    And nothing 'gainst Time's scythe can
        make defence,
    Save breed, to brave him, when he takes
        thee hence.

SHALL I compare thee to a summer's day?
Thou art more lovely and more temperate;
Rough winds do shake the darling buds of
    May.
And summer's lease hath all too short a
    date.
Sometime too hot the eye of heaven shines,
And often is his gold complexion dimmed,
And every fair from fair sometime declines,
By chance, or nature's changing course,
    untrimmed;
But thy eternal summer shall not fade,
Nor lose possession of that fair thou owest;
Nor shall death brag thou wander'st in his
    shade,
When in eternal lines to time thou growest.
    So long as men can breathe, or eyes can
        see,
    So long lives this, and this gives life to
        thee.

So is it not with me as with that Muse,
Stirred by a painted beauty to his verse;
Who heaven itself for ornament doth use,
And every fair with his fair doth rehearse;
Making a compliment of proud compare,
With sun and moon, with earth and sea's
    rich gems,
With April's first-born flowers, and all
    things rare
That heaven's air in this huge rondure
    hems.

Oh let me, true in love, but truly write,
And then believe me, my love is as fair
As any mother's child, though not so bright
As those gold candles fixed in heaven's air:
    Let them say no more that like of hear-
        say well;
    I will not praise, that purpose not to sell.

LET those who are in favor with their stars,
Of public honor and proud titles boast;
Whilst I, whom fortune of such triumphs
    bars;
Unlooked-for joy in that I honor most.
Great princes favorites their fair leaves
    spread,
But as the marigold, at the sun's eye;
And in themselves their pride lies buried,
For at a frown they in their glory die.
The painful warrior famoused for fight,
After a thousand victories once foiled,
Is from the book of honor rased quite,
And all the rest forgot for which he toiled.
    Then happy I, that love and am beloved,
    Where I may not remove nor be removed.

WHEN in disgrace with fortune and men's
    eyes,
I all alone beweep my outcast state,
And trouble deaf heaven with my bootless
    cries,
And look upon myself, and curse my fate,
Wishing me like to one more rich in hope,
Featured like him, like him with friends
    possessed,
Desiring this man's art, and that man's
    scope,
With what I most enjoy contented least;
Yet in these thoughts myself almost
    despising,
Haply I think on thee, and then my state
(Like to the lark at break of day arising
From sullen earth) sings hymns at heaven's
    gate.
    For thy sweet love remembered such
        wealth brings,
    That then I scorn to change my state
        with kings.

WHEN to the sessions of sweet silent
    thought
I summon up remembrance of things past,
I sigh the lack of many a thing I sought,
And with old woes new wail my dear
    time's waste.
Then, can I drown an eye, unused to flow,
-For precious friends hid in death's dateless
    night,
And weep afresh love's long since cancelled
    woe,
And moan th' expense of many a vanished
    sight.
Then can I grieve of grievances foregone,
And heavily from woe to woe tell o'er
The sad account of fore-bemoaned moan,
Which I new pay, as if not paid before:
But if the while I think on thee, dear
    friend,
All losses are restored, and sorrow ends.

———

THY bosom is endeared with all hearts,
Which I by lacking have supposed dead;
And there reigns love, and all love's loving
    parts,
And all those friends which I thought
    buried.
How many a holy and obsequious tear
Hath dear religious love stol'n from mine
    eye,
As interest of the dead, which now appear
But things removed, that hidden in thee lie!
Thou art the grave where buried love doth
    live,
Hung with the trophies of my lovers gone,
Who all their parts of me to thee did give;
That due of many now is thine alone:
    Their images I loved I view in thee,
    And thou (all they) hast all the all of me.

———

FULL many a glorious morning have I seen
Flatter tne mountain tops with sovereign
    eye,
Kissing with golden face the meadows
    green,

Gilding pale streams with heavenly al-
    chemy;
Anon permit the basest clouds to ride
With ugly rack on his celestial face,
And from the forlorn world his visage hide,
Stealing unseen to west with this disgrace.
Even so my sun one early morn did shine,
With all triumphant splendor on my brow;
But out, alack! he was but one hour mine,
The region cloud hath masked him from
    me now.
    Yet him for this my love no whit dis-
        daineth;
    Suns of the world may stain, when heav-
        en's sun staineth.

———

WHY didst thou promise such a beauteous
    day,
And make me travel forth without my
    cloak,
To let base clouds o'ertake me in my way,
Hiding thy bravery in their rotten smoke?
'T is not enough that through the cloud
    thou break,
To dry the rain on my storm-beaten face,
For no man well of such a salve can speak,
That heals the wound, and cures not the
    disgrace;
Nor can thy shame give physic to my
    grief—
Though thou repent, yet I have still the
    loss:
Th' offender's sorrow lends but weak relief
To him that bears the strong offence's
    cross,
    Ah, but those tears are pearl, which thy
        love sheds,
    And they are rich, and ransom all ill
        deeds.

———

WHAT is your substance, whereof are you
    made,
That millions of strange shadows on you
    tend?
Since every one hath, every one, one shade,
And you, but one, can every shadow lend.

Describe Adonis, and the counterfeit
Is poorly imitated after you;
On Helen's cheek all art of beauty set,
And you in Grecian tires are painted new:
Speak of the spring, and foison of the year—
The one doth shadow of your beauty show,
The other as your bounty doth appear;
And you in every blessed shape we know.
  In all external grace you have some part;
  But you like none, none you, for constant
    heart.

———

Oh, how much more doth beauty beauteous
    seem,
By that sweet ornament which truth doth
    give!
The rose looks fair, but fairer we it deem
For that sweet odor which doth in it live.
The canker-blooms have full as deep a dye
As the perfumed tincture of the roses—
Hang on such thorns, and play as wantonly
When summer's breath their masked buds
    discloses;
But, for their virtue only is their show;
They live unwooed, and unrespected fade,
Die to themselves. Sweet roses do not so;
Of their sweet deaths are sweetest odors
  made:
    And so of you beauteous and lovely
      youth,
    When that shall fade, my verse distils
      your truth.

———

Not marble, nor the gilded monuments
Of princes, shall outlive this powerful
    rhyme,
But you shall shine more bright in these
    contents
Than unswept stone, besmeared with slut-
    tish time.
When wasteful war shall statues overturn,
And broils root out the works of masonry,
Nor Mars his sword, nor war's quick fire
    shall burn
The living record of your memory.

'Gainst death and all oblivious enmity
Shall you pace forth: your praise shall still
    find room
Even in the eyes of all posterity,
That wear this world out to the ending
    doom.
  So, till the judgment that yourself arise,
  You live in this, and dwell in lover's
    eyes.

        Willam Shakespeare.

———

THE MOTHER'S HOPE.

Is there, when the winds are singing
  In the happy summer time—
When the raptured air is ringing
With earth's music heavenward springing,
  Forest chirp, and village chime—
Is there, of the sounds that float
Unsighingly, a single note
Half so sweet, and clear, and wild,
As the laughter of a child?

Listen! and be now delighted:
  Morn hath touched her golden strings;
Earth and Sky their vows have plighted;
Life and Light are reunited,
  Amid countless carollings;
Yet, delicious as they are,
There's a sound that's sweeter far—
One that makes the heart rejoice
More than all,—the human voice!

Organ finer, deeper, clearer,
Though it be a stranger's tone—
Than the winds or waters dearer,
More enchanting to the hearer,
  For it answereth to his own
But, of all its witching words,
Those are sweetest, bubbling wild
Through the laughter of a child.

Harmonies from time-touched towers,
  Haunted strains from rivulets,
Hum of bees among the flowers,
Rustling leaves, and silver showers,—
  These, ere long, the ear forgets;

But in mine there is a sound
Ringing on the whole year round—
Heart-deep laughter that I heard
Ere my child could speak a word.

Ah! 't was heard by ear far purer,
  Fondlier formed to catch the strain—
Ear of one whose love is surer—
Hers, the mother, the endurer
  Of the deepest share of pain;
Hers the deepest bliss to treasure
Memories of that cry of pleasure;
Hers to hoard, a life-time after,
Echoes of that infant laughter.

'T is a mother's large affection
  Hears with a mysterious sense—
Breathings that evade detection,
Whisper faint, and fine inflexion,
  Thrill in her with power intense.
Childhood's honeyed words untaught
Hiveth she in loving thought—
Tones that never thence depart;
For she listens—with her heart.

Laman Blanchard.

FLEURETTE.

We have been friends together,
  In sunshine and in shade,
Since first beneath the chestnut-tree
  In infancy we played;
But coldness dwells within thy heart,
  A cloud is on thy brow;
We have been friends together,—
  Shall a light word part us now?

We have been gay together;
  We have laughed at little jests;
For the fount of hope was gushing,
  Warm and joyous, in our breasts.
But laughter now hath fled thy lip,
  And sullen glooms thy brow
We have been gay together,—
  Shall a light word part us now?

We have been sad together,—
  We have wept, with bitter tears,
O'er the grass-grown graves, where slum-
    bered
  The hopes of early years.
The voices which are silent there
  Would bid thee clear thy brow;
We have been sad together,—
  O, what shall part us now?

Caroline Elizabeth Sarah Norton.

THE MOTHER'S HEART.

When first thou camest, gentle, shy, and
    fond,
  My eldest born, first hope, and dearest
    treasure,
My heart received thee with a joy beyond
  All that it yet had felt of earthly pleasure;
Nor thought that any love again might be
So deep and strong as that I felt for thee.

Faithful and true, with sense beyond thy
    years,
  And natural piety that leaned to heaven;
Wrung by a harsh word suddenly to tears,
  Yet patient to rebuke when justly
    given—
Obedient—easy to be reconciled—
And meekly cheerful; such wert thou, my
    child!

Not willing to be left—still by my side,
  Haunting my walks, while summer-day
    was dying;
Nor leaving in thy turn, but pleased to
    glide
  Through the dark room where I was
    sadly lying;
Or by the couch of pain, a sitter meek,
Watch the dim eye, and kiss the fevered
    cheek.

O boy! of such as thou are oftenest made
  Earth's fragile idols, like a tender flower,
No strength in all thy freshness, prone to
    fade,

FLEURETTE.

And bending weakly to the thunder-
shower;
Still, round the loved, thy heart found force
to bind,
And clung, like woodbine shaken in the
wind!

Then THOU, my merry love—bold in thy
glee,
Under the bough, or by the firelight
dancing,
With thy sweet temper, and thy spirit free—
Didst come, as restless as a bird's wing
glancing,
Full of a wild and irrepressible mirth,
Like a young sunbeam to the gladdened
earth!

Thine was the shout, the song, the burst of
joy,
Which sweet from childhood's rosy lips
resoundeth;
Thine was the eager spirit naught could
cloy,
And the glad heart from which all grief
reboundeth;
And many a mirthful jest and mock reply
Lurked in the laughter of thy dark-blue eye.

And thine was many an art to win and
bless,
The cold and stern to joy and fondness
warming;
The coaxing smile — the frequent soft
caress—
The earnest tearful prayer all wrath dis-
arming!
Again my heart a new affection found,
But thought that love with thee had
reached its bound.

At length THOU camest—thou, the last and
least,
Nick-named "the Emperor" by thy
laughing brothers—
Because a haughty spirit swelled thy breast,
And thou didst seek to rule and sway the
others—
Mingling with every playful infant wile
A mimic majesty that made us smile.

And oh! most like a regal child wert thou!
An eye of resolute and successful schem-
ing!
Fair shoulders—curling lips—and daunt-
less brow—
Fit for the world's strife, not for poet's
dreaming;
And proud the lifting of thy stately head,
And the firm bearing of thy conscious
tread.

Different from both! yet each succeeding
claim
I, that all other love had been forswear-
ing,
Forthwith admitted, equal and the same;
Nor injured either by this love's compar-
ing,
Nor stole a fraction for the newer call—
But in the mother's heart found room for
all!

CAROLINE NORTON.

LOVE.

LOVE? I will tell you what it is to love!
It is to build with human thoughts a shrine,
Where Hope sits brooding like a beauteous
dove,
Where Time seems young, and Life a
thing divine.
All tastes, all pleasures, all desires combine
To consecrate this sanctuary of bliss.
Above, the stars in cloudless beauty shine;
Around, the streams their flowery margins
kiss;
And if there's heaven on earth, that heaven
is surely this.

Yes, this is Love, the steadfast and the
true,
The immortal glory which hath never set;
The best, the brightest boon the heart e'er
knew:
Of all life's sweets the very sweetest yet!
O! who but can recall the eve they met
To breathe, in some green walk, their first
young vow?

While summer flowers with moonlight
    dews were wet,
And winds sighed soft around the moun-
    tain's brow,
And all was rapture then which is but
    memory now!
            CHARLES SWAIN.

CHRISTINE.

I LOVED him not; and yet, now he is gone,
    I feel I am alone.
I checked him while he spoke: yet could
    he speak,
    Alas! I would not check.
For reasons not to love him once I sought,
    And wearied all my thought
To vex myself and him: I now would give
    My love could he but live
Who lately lived for me, and when he
    found
    'T was vain, in holy ground
He hid his face amid the shades of death!
    I waste for him my breath
Who wasted his for me; but mine returns,
    And this lone bosom burns
With stifling heat, heaving it up in sleep,
    And waking me to weep
Tears that had melted his soft heart: for
    years
    Wept he as bitter tears!
"Merciful God!" such was his latest prayer,
    "These may she never share!"
Quieter in his breath, his breath more cold
    Than daisies in the mold,
Where children spell athwart the church-
    yard gate
    His name and life's brief date.
Pray for him, gentle souls, whoe'er ye be,
    And O, pray, too, for me!
        —WALTER SAVAGE LANDOR.

LOCKSLEY HALL.

COMRADES, leave me here a little, while as
    yet 't is early morn—
Leave me here, and when you want me,
    sound upon the bugle horn.

'T is the place, and all around it, as of old,
    the curlews call,
Dreary gleams about the moorland, flying
    over Locksley Hall;

Locksley Hall, that in the distance over-
    looks the sandy tracts,
And the hollow ocean-ridges roaring into
    cataracts.

Many a night from yonder ivied casement,
    ere I went to rest,
Did I look on great Orion sloping slowly
    to the west.

Many a night I saw the Pleiads, rising
    through the mellow shade,
Glitter like a swarm of fire-flies tangled in
    a silver braid.

Here about the beach I wandered, nourish-
    ing a youth sublime
With the fairy tales of science, and the long
    result of time;

When the centuries behind me like a fruit-
    ful land reposed;
When I clung to all the present for the
    promise that it closed;

When I dipt into the future far as human
    eye could see—
Saw the vision of the world, and all the
    wonder that would be.

In the spring a fuller crimson comes upon
    the robin's breast;
In the spring the wanton lapwing gets him-
    self another crest;

In the spring a livelier iris changes on the
    burnished dove;
In the spring a young man's fancy lightly
    turns to thoughts of love.

Then her cheek was pale and thinner than
    should be for one so young,
And her eyes on all my motions with a
    mute observance hung.

CHRISTINE.

And I said, "My cousin Amy, speak, and
speak the truth to me;
Trust me, cousin, all the current of my
being sets to thee."

On her pallid cheek and forehead came a
color and a light,
As I have seen the rosy red flushing in the
northern night.

And she turned—her bosom shaken with a
sudden storm of sighs—'
All the spirit deeply dawning in the dark
of hazel eyes—

Saying, "I have hid my feelings, fearing
they should do me wrong;"
Saying, "Dost thou love me, cousin?"
weeping, "I have loved thee long."

Love took up the glass of time, and turned
it in his glowing hands;
Every moment, lightly shaken, ran itself in
golden sands.

Love took up the harp of life, and smote
on all the chords with might;
Smote the chord of self, that, trembling,
passed in music out of sight.

Many a morning on the moorland did we
hear the copses ring,
And her whisper thronged my pulses with
the fulness of the spring.

Many an evening by the waters did we
watch the stately ships,
And our spirits rushed together at the
touching of the lips.

O my cousin, shallow-hearted! Oh my
Amy, mine no more!
Oh the dreary, dreary moorland! Oh the
barren, barren shore!

Falser than all fancy fathoms, falser than
all songs have sung—
Puppet to a father's threat, and servile to a
shrewish tongue!

Is it well to wish thee happy?—having
known me; to decline
On a range of lower feelings and a narrower
heart than mine!

Yet it shall be: thou shalt lower to his level
day by day,
What is fine within thee growing coarse to
sympathize with clay.

As the husband is, the wife is; thou art
mated with a clown,
And the grossness of his nature will have
weight to drag thee down.

He will hold thee, when his passion shall
have spent its novel force,
Something better than his dog, a little
dearer than his horse.

What is this? his eyes are heavy—think
not they are glazed with wine.
Go to him; it is thy duty—kiss him; take
his hand in thine.

It may be my lord is weary, that his brain
is overwrought—
Soothe him with thy finer fancies, touch
him with thy lighter thought.

He will answer to the purpose, easy things
to understand—
Better thou wert dead before me, though I
slew thee with my hands.

Better thou and I were lying, hidden from
the heart's disgrace,
Rolled in one another's arms, and silent in
a last embrace.

Cursed be the social wants that sin against
the strength of youth!
Cursed be the social lies that warp us from
the living truth!

Cursed be the sickly forms that err from
honest nature's rule!
Cursed be the gold that gilds the straitened
forehead of the fool!

Well—'t is well that I should bluster!—
Hadst thou less unworthy proved,
Would to God—for I had loved thee more
than ever wife was loved.

Am I mad, that I should cherish that which
bears but bitter fruit?
I will pluck it from my bosom, though my
heart be at the root.

Never! though my mortal summers to such
length of years should come
As the many-wintered crow that leads the
clanging rookery home.

Where is comfort? in division of the records
of the mind?
Can I part her from herself, and love her,
as I knew her, kind?

I remember one that perished; sweetly did
she speak and move;
Such a one do I remember, whom to look
at was to love.

Can I think of her as dead, and love her
for the love she bore?
No—she never loved me truly; love is love
for evermore.

Comfort? comfort scorned of devils! this
is truth the poet sings,
That a sorrow's crown of sorrow is remem-
bering happier things.

Drug thy memories, lest thou learn it, lest
thy heart be put to proof,
In the dead, unhappy night, and when the
rain is on the roof.

Like a dog, he hunts in dreams; and thou
art staring at the wall,
Where the dying night-lamp flickers, and
the shadows rise and fall.

Then a hand shall pass before thee, pointing to his drunken sleep,
To thy widowed marriage-pillows, to the
tears that thou wilt weep.

Thou shalt hear the "Never, never," whispered by the phantom years,
And a song from out the distance in the
ringing of thine ears;

And an eye shall vex thee, looking ancient
kindness on thy pain.
Turn thee, turn thee on thy pillow; get
thee to thy rest again.

Nay, but nature brings thee solace; for a
tender voice will cry;
'T is a purer life than thine; a lip to drain
thy trouble dry.

Baby lips will laugh me down; my latest
rival brings thee rest—
Baby fingers, waxen touches, press me
from the mother's breast.

Oh, the child, too, clothes the father with a
dearness not his due;
Half is thine, and half is his—it will be
worthy of the two.

Oh, I see thee, old and formal, fitted to thy
petty part,
With a little hoard of maxims preaching
down a daughter's heart:

"They were dangerous guides, the feelings—she herself was not exempt—
Truly, she herself had suffered."—Perish
in thy self-contempt!

Overlive it—lower yet—be happy! wherefore should I care?
I myself must mix with action, lest I
wither by despair.

What is that which I should turn to, light-
ing upon days like these?
Every door is barred with gold, and opens
but to golden keys.

Every gate is thronged with suitors; all the
markets overflow.
I have but an angry fancy: what is that
which I should do?

I had been content to perish, falling on the foeman's ground,
When the ranks are rolled in vapor, and the winds are laid with sound.

But the jingling of the guinea helps the hurt that honor feels,
And the nations do but murmur, snarling at each other's heels.

Can I but relive in sadness? I will turn that earlier page.
Hide me from my deep emotion, O thou wondrous mother-age!

Make me feel the wild pulsation that I felt before the strife,
When I heard my days before me, and the tumult of my life;

Yearning for the large excitement that the coming years would yield—
Eager-hearted as a boy when first he leaves his father's field,

And at night along the dusky highway near and nearer drawn,
Sees in heaven the light of London flaring like a dreary dawn;

And his spirit leaps within him to be gone before him then,
Underneath the light he looks at, in among the throngs of men—

Men, my brothers, men the workers, ever reaping something new:
That which they have done but earnest of the things that they shall do;

For I dipt into the future, as far as human eye could see—
Saw the vision of the world, and all the wonder that would be—

Saw the heavens fill with commerce, argosies of magic sails,
Pilots of the purple twilight, dropping down with costly bales—

Heard the heavens fill with shouting, and there rained a ghastly dew
From the nation's airy navies grappling in the central blue;

Far along the world-wide whisper of the south-wind rushing warm,
With the standards of the peoples plunging through the thunder storm;

Till the war-drum throbbed no longer, and the battle-flags were furled
In the parliament of man, the federation of the world.

There the common sense of most shall hold a fretful realm in awe,
And the kindly earth shall slumber, lapt in universal law.

So I triumphed, ere my passion sweeping through me, left me dry,
Left me with a palsied heart, and left me with the jaundiced eye—

Eye, to which all order festers, all things here are out of joint.
Silence moves, but slowly, slowly, creeping on from point to point;

Slowly comes a hungry people, as a lion, creeping nigher,
Glares at one that nods and winks behind a slowly-dying fire.

Yet I doubt not through the ages one increasing purpose runs,
And the thoughts of men are widened with the process of the suns.

What is that to him that reaps not harvest of his youthful joys,
Though the deep heart of existence beat for ever like a boy's?

Knowledge comes, but wisdom lingers; and I linger on the shore,
And the individual withers, and the world is more and more.

Knowledge blinds, but wisdom lingers, and
    he bears a laden breast,
Full of sad experience moving toward the
    stillness of his rest.

Hark! my merry comrades call me, sound-
    ing on the bugle horn—
They to whom my foolish passion were a
    target for their scorn;

Shall it not be scorn to me to harp on such
    a mouldered string?
I am ashamed through all my nature to
    have loved so slight a thing.

Weakness to be wroth with weakness!
    woman's pleasure, woman's pain—
Nature made them blinder motions bound-
    ed in a shallower brain;

Woman is the lesser man, and all thy pas-
    sions, matched with mine,
Are as moonlight unto sunlight, and as
    water unto wine—

Here at least, where nature sickens, noth-
    ing. Ah, for some retreat
Deep in yonder shining orient, where my
    life began to beat

Where in wild Mahratta-battle fell my
    father, evil-starred;
I was left a trampled orphan, and a selfish
    uncle's ward.

Or to burst all links of habit—there to
    wander far away,
On from island unto island at the gate-
    ways of the day—

Larger constellations burning, mellow
    moons and happy skies,
Breadths of tropic shade and palms in clus-
    ter, knots of Paradise

Never comes the trader, never floats an
    European flag—
Slides the bird o'er lustrous woodland,
    droops the trailer from the crag—

Droops the heavy-blossomed bower, hangs
    the heavy-fruited tree—
Summer isles of Eden lying in dark-purple
    spheres of sea.

There, methinks, would be enjoyment more
    than in this march of mind—
In the steamship, in the railway, in the
    thoughts that shake mankind.

There the passions, cramped no longer,
    shall have scope and breathing-space;
I will take some savage woman, she shall
    rear my dusky race.

Iron-jointed, supple-sinewed, they shall
    dive, and they shall run,
Catch the wild goat by the hair, and hurl
    their lances in the sun.

Whistle back the parrot's call, and leap the
    rainbows of the brooks,
Not with blinded eyesight poring over mis-
    erable books—

Fool, again the dream, the fancy! but I
    know my words are wild,
But I count the gray barbarian lower than
    the Christian child.

I, to herd with narrow foreheads, vacant of
    our glorious gains,
Like a beast with lower pleasures, like a
    beast with lower pains!

Mated with a squalid savage—what to me
    were sun or clime?
I, the heir of all the ages, in the foremost
    files of time—

I, that rather held it better men should
    perish one by one,
Than that earth should stand at gaze like
    Joshua's moon in Ajalon!

Not in vain the distance beacons. For-
    ward let us range;
Let the great world spin forever down the
    ringing grooves of change.

Through the shadow of the globe we sweep
 into the younger day :
Better fifty years of Europe than a cycle of
 Cathay.

Mother-age, (for mine I knew not,) help
 me as when life begun—
Rift the hills, and roll the waters, flash the
 lightnings, weigh the sun—

Oh, I see the crescent promise of my spirit
 hath not set;
Ancient founts of inspiration well through
 all my fancy yet.

Howsoever these things be, a long farewell
 to Locksley Hall!
Now for me the woods may wither, now
 for me the roof-tree fall.

Comes a vapor from the margin, blacken-
 ing over heath and holt,
Cramming all the blast before it, in its
 breast a thunderbolt.

Let it fall on Locksley Hall, with rain or
 hail, or fire or snow;
For the mighty wind arises, roaring sea-
 ward, and I go.

ALFRED TENNYSON.

———

THE END OF THE PLAY.

THE play is done—the curtain drops,
 Slow falling to the prompter's bell;
A moment yet the actor stops,
 And looks around, to say farewell.
It is an irksome word and task;
 And, when he 's laughed and said his say,
He shows, as he removes the mask,
 A face that 's any thing but gay.

One word, ere yet the evening ends—
 Let 's close it with a parting rhyme;
And pledge a hand to all young friends,
 As fits the merry Christmas time;

On life's wide scene you, too, have parts,
 That fate ere long shall bid you play;
Good-night!—with honest gentle hearts
 A kindly greeting go alway!

Good-night!—I 'd say the griefs, the joys,
 Just hinted in this mimic page,
The triumphs and defeats of boys,
 Are but repeated in our age;
I 'd say your woes were not less keen,
 Your hopes more vain, than those of men
Your pangs or pleasures of fifteen
 At forty-five played o'er again.

I 'd say we suffer and we strive
 Not less nor more as men than boys—
With grizzled beards at forty-five,
 As erst at twelve in corduroys;
And if, in time of sacred youth,
 We learned at home to love and pray,
Pray heaven that early love and truth
 May never wholly pass away.

And in the world, as in the school,
 I 'd say how fate may change and shift—
The prize be sometimes with the fool,
 The race not always to the swift;
The strong may yield, the good may fall,
 The great man be a vulgar clown,
The knave be lifted over all,
 The kind cast pitilessly down.

Who knows the inscrutable design?
 Blessed be He who took and gave!
Why should your mother, Charles, not
 mine,
 Be weeping at her darling's grave?
We bow to heaven that willed it so,
 . That darkly rules the fate of all,
That sends the respite or the blow,
 That 's free to give or to recall.

This crowns his feast with wine and wit—
 Who brought him to that mirth and
 state?
His betters, see, below him sit,
 Or hunger hopeless at the gate.
Who bade the mud from Dives' wheel
 To spurn the rags of Lazarus?

Come, brother, in that dust we 'll kneel,
Confessing heaven that ruled it thus.

So each shall mourn, in life's advance,
Dear hopes, dear friends, untimely
killed—
Shall grieve for many a forfeit chance,
And longing passion unfulfilled.
Amen!—whatever fate be sent,
Pray God the heart may kindly glow,
Although the head with cares be bent,
And whitened with the winter snow.

Come wealth or want, come good or ill,
Let old and young accept their part,
And bow before the awful will,
And bear it with an honest heart.
Who misses, or who wins the prize—
Go, lose or conquer as you can;
But if you fail, or if you rise,
Be each, pray God, a gentleman.

A gentleman, or old or young!
(Bear kindly with my humble lays;)
The sacred chorus first was sung
Upon the first of Christmas days;
The shepherds heard it overhead—
The joyful angels raised it then:
Glory to heaven on high, it said,
And peace on earth to gentle men!

My song, save this, is little worth;
I lay the weary pen aside,
And wish you health, and love, and mirth,
As fits the solemn Christmas-tide.
As fits the holy Christmas birth,
Be this, good friends, our carol still—
Be peace on earth, be peace on earth,
To men of gentle will.

WILLIAM MAKEPEACE THACKERAY.

WOODMAN, SPARE THAT TREE.

Woodman, spare that tree!
Touch not a single bough!
In youth it sheltered me,
And I 'll protect it now.

'T was my forfather's hand
That placed it near his cot;
There, woodman, let it stand,
Thy axe shall harm it not!

That old familiar tree,
Whose glory and renown
Are spread o'er land and sea,
And wouldst thou hew it down?
Woodman, forbear thy stroke!
Cut not its earth-bound ties;
O, spare that aged oak,
Now towering to the skies!

When but an idle boy
I sought its grateful shade;
In all their gushing joy
Here too my sisters played.
My mother kissed me here;
My father pressed my hand—
Forgive this foolish tear,
But let that old oak stand!

My heart strings round thee cling,
Close as thy bark, old friend!
Here shall the wild bird sing,
And still thy branches bend.
Old tree! the storm still brave!
And, woodman, leave the spot;
While I 've a hand to save,
Thy axe shall harm it not.

GEORGE P. MORRIS.

THE MISTLETOE BOUGH.

The mistletoe hung in the castle hall,
The holly branch shone on the old oak
wall;
And the Baron's retainers were blithe and
gay,
And keeping their Christmas holiday.
The Baron beheld with a father's pride
His beautiful child, young Lovell's bride;
While she with her bright eyes seemed to
be
The star of the goodly company.

THE MISTLETOE BOUGH.

"I 'm weary of dancing now," she cried;
'Here tarry a moment,—I 'll hide, I 'll hide !
And, Lovell, be sure, thou 'rt first to trace
The clew to my secret lurking-place "
Away she ran—and her friends began
Each tower to search, and each nook to
  scan;
And young Lovell cried, "O, where dost
  thou hide?
I 'm lonesome without thee, my own dear
  bride."

They sought her that night, and they
  sought her next day,
And they sought her in vain when a week
  passed away,
In the highest, the lowest, the loneliest
  spot,
Young Lovell sought wildly,—but found
  her not,
And years flew by, and their grief at last
Was told as a sorrowful tale long past,
And when Lovell appeared, the children
  cried,
"See! the old man weeps for his fairy
  bride."

At length an oak chest that had long laid
  hid,
Was found in the castle,—they raised the
  lid,
And a skeleton form lay mouldering there
In the bridal wreath of that lady fair!
O, sad was her fate!—in sportive jest
She hid from her lord in the old oak chest.
It closed with a spring!—and dreadful
  doom,
The bride lay clasped in her living tomb!

        THOMAS HAYNES BAYLY.

TO PERILLA.

AH, my Perilla! dost thou grieve to see
Me, day by day, to steal away from thee?
Age calls me hence, and my gray hairs bid
  come,
And haste away to mine eternal home;

'T will not not be long, Perilla, after this
That I must give thee the supremest kiss.
Dead when I am, first cast in salt, and
  bring
Part of the cream from that religious
  spring,
With which, Perilla, wash my hands and
  feet;
That done, then wind me in that very
  sheet
Which wrapped thy smooth limbs when
  thou didst implore
The gods' protection, but the night before;
Follow me weeping to my turf, and there
Let fall a primrose, and with it a tear.
Then lastly, let some weekly strewings be
Devoted to the memory of me;
Then shall my ghost not walk about, but
  keep
Still in the cool and silent shades of sleep.

        ROBERT HERRICK.

THE ONE GRAY HAIR.

THE wisest of the wise
Listen to pretty lies,
  And love to hear them told;
Doubt not that Solomon
Listened to many a one—
Some in his youth, and more when he grew
  old.

I never sat among
The choir of wisdom's song,
  But pretty lies loved I
As much as any king—
When youth was on the wing,
And (must it then be told?) when youth
  had quite gone by.

Alas! and I have not
The pleasant hour forgot,
  When one pert lady said—
"O, Landor! I am quite
Bewildered with affright;
I see (sit quiet now!) a white hair on your
  head!"

Another, more benign,
Drew out that hair of mine,
   And in her own dark hair
Pretended she had found
That one, and twirled it round.
Fair as she was, she never was so fair.
          WALTER SAVAGE LANDOR.

MEMORY.

The mother of the muses, we are taught,
Is memory, she has left me: they remain,
And shake my shoulder, urging me to sing
About the summer days, my loves of old.
" Alas! alas!" is all I can reply.
Memory has left with me that name alone,
Harmonious name, which other bards may
     sing,
But her bright image in my darkest hour
Comes back, in vain comes back, called or
     uncalled.
Forgotten are the names of visitors
Ready to press my hand but yesterday;
Forgotten are the names of earlier friends
Whose genial converse and glad counte-
     nance
Are fresh as ever to mine ear and eye;
To these, when I have written, and
     besought
Remembrance of me, the word " Dear "
     alone
Hangs on the upper verge, and waits in
     vain.
A blessing wert thou, O oblivion,
If thy stream carried only weeds away,
But vernal and autumnal flowers alike
It hurries down to wither on the strand,
          WALTER SAVAGE LANDOR.

THE RAVEN.

ONCE, upon a midnight dreary, while I
     pondered, weak and weary,
Over many a quaint and curious volume
     of forgotten lore—
While I nodded, nearly napping, suddenly
     there came a tapping,

As of some one gently rapping, rapping at
     my chamber door:
" 'T is some visitor," I muttered, " tapping
     at my chamber door—
     Only this, and nothing more."

Ah! distinctly I remember! it was in the
     bleak December,
And each separate dying ember wrought
     its ghost upon the floor.
Eagerly I wished the morrow; vainly I had
     tried to borrow
From my books surcease of sorrow—sor-
     row for the lost Lenore—
For the rare and radiant maiden whom the
     angels name Lenore—
     Nameless here for evermore.

And the silken, sad, uncertain rustling of
     each purple curtain
Thrilled me—filled me with fantastic ter-
     rors never felt before:
So that now, to still the beating of my
     heart, I stood repeating,
" 'T is some visitor entreating entrance at
     my chamber door;—
     This it is, and nothing more."

Presently my soul grew stronger; hesitat-
     ing then no longer,
" Sir," said I, " or madam, truly your for-
     giveness I implore;
But the fact is I was napping, and so gently
     you came rapping,
And so faintly you came tapping, tapping
     at my chamber door,
That I scarce was sure I heard you,"—here
     I opened wide the door:
     Darkness there, and nothing more!

Deep into that darkness peering, long I
     stood there wondering, fearing,
Doubting, dreaming dreams no mortal ever
     dared to dream before;
But the silence was unbroken, and the
     darkness gave no token,
And the only word there spoken was the
     whispered word, " Lenore!"
This I whispered, and an echo murmured
     back the word " Lenore!"
     Merely this, and nothing more.

Then into the chamber turning, all my soul
    within me burning,
Soon I heard again a tapping, somewhat
    louder than before:
"Surely," said I, "surely that is something
    at my window lattice;
Let me see, then, what thereat is, and this
    mystery explore:—
Let my heart be still a moment, and this
    mystery explore;—
       'T is the wind, and nothing more!"

Open here I flung the shutter, when, with
    many a flirt and flutter,
In there stepped a stately raven of the
    saintly days of yore;
Not the least obeisance made he; not an in-
    stant stopped or stayed he;
But, with mien of lord or lady, perched
    above my chamber door—
Perched upon a bust of Pallas, just above
    my chamber door—
       Perched, and sat, and nothing more.

Then this ebony bird beguiling my sad
    fancy into smiling,
By the grave and stern decorum of the
    countenance it wore;
" Though thy crest be shorn and shaven,
    thou," I said, " art sure no craven—
Ghastly, grim and ancient raven, wander-
    ing from the nightly shore—
Tell me what thy lordly name is on the
    night's Plutonian shore!"
       Quoth the raven, " Nevermore."

Much I marvelled this ungainly fowl to
    hear discourse so plainly—
Though its answer little meaning, little
    relevancy bore;
For we cannot help agreeing that no living
    human being
Ever yet was blessed with seeing bird above
    his chamber door—
Bird or beast upon the sculptured bust
    above his chamber door,
       With such name as " Nevermore."

But the raven, sitting lonely on the placid
    bust, spoke only

That one word, as if his soul in that one
    word he did outpour.
Nothing farther then he uttered—not a
    feather then he fluttered—
Till I scarcely more than muttered, "Other
    friends have flown before—
On the morrow he will leave me, as my
    hopes have flown before."
       Then the bird said, " Nevermore."

Startled at the stillness broken by reply so
    aptly spoken,
" Doubtless," said I, " what it utters is its
    only stock and store—
Caught from some unhappy master, whom
    unmerciful disaster
Followed fast and followed faster, till his
    songs one burden bore—
Till the dirges of his hope the melancholy
    burden bore
       Of ' Never—Nevermore.' "

But the raven still beguiling all my sad
    soul into smiling,
Straight I wheeled a cushioned seat in front
    of bird, and bust and door;
Then upon the velvet sinking, I betook
    myself to linking
Fancy unto fancy, thinking what this om-
    inous bird of yore—
What this grim, ungainly, ghastly, gaunt,
    and ominous bird of yore
       Meant in croaking " Nevermore."

This I sat engaged in guessing, but no syl-
    lable expressing
To the fowl, whose fiery eyes now burned
    into my bosom's core;
This, and more, I sat divining, with my
    head at ease reclining,
On the cushion's velvet lining that the
    lamplight gloated o'er;
But whose velvet violet lining, with the
    lamplight gloating o'er,
       She shall press—ah, never more!

Then, methought, the air grew denser,
    perfumed from an unseen censer
Swung by angels, whose faint foot-falls
    tinkled on the tufted floor.

"Wretch!" I cried, "thy God hath lent
  thee, by these angels he hath sent thee,
Respite—respite and nepenthe from thy
  memories of Lenore!
Quaff, oh quaff this kind nepenthe, and forget this lost Lenore!"
      Quoth the raven, "Nevermore."

"Prophet!" said I, thing of evil!—prophet
  still, if bird or devil!
Whether tempter sent, or whether tempest
  tossed thee here ashore—
Desolate, yet all undaunted, on this desert
  land enchanted,
On this home by horror haunted—tell me
  truly, I implore—
Is there—is there balm in Gilead? tell me—
  tell me, I implore!"
      Quoth the raven, "Nevermore."

"Prophet!" said I, "thing of evil!—prophet
  still, if bird or devil!
By that heaven that bends above us—by
  that God we both adore—
Tell this soul with sorrow laden if, within
  the distant Aidenn,
It shall clasp a sainted maiden whom the
  angels name Lenore—
Clasp a rare and radiant maiden whom the
  angels name Lenore."
      Quoth the raven, "Nevermore."

"Be that word our sign of parting, bird or
  fiend!" I shrieked, upstarting—
"Get thee back into the tempest and the
  night's Plutonian shore!
Leave no black plume as a token of that
  lie thy soul hath spoken!
Leave my loneliness unbroken!—quit the
  bust above my door!
Take thy beak from out my heart, and take
  thy form from off my door!"
      Quoth the raven, "Nevermore."

And the raven, never flitting, still is sitting,
  still is sitting
On the pallid bust of Pallas just above my
  chamber door;

And his eyes have all the seeming of a demon's that is dreaming,
And the lamplight, o'er him streaming
  throws his shadow on the floor;
And my soul from out that shadow that
  lies floating on the floor
      Shall be lifted—nevermore!
                    EDGAR ALLAN POE.

———

SONG OF THE WINDS.

Up the dale and down the bourne,
  O'er the meadow swift we fly;
Now we sing, and now we mourn,
  Now we whistle, now we sigh.

By the grassy-fringed river,
  Through the murmuring reeds we sweep;
Mid the lily-leaves we quiver,
  To their very hearts we creep.

Now the maiden rose is blushing
  At the frolic things we say,
While aside her cheek we 're rushing;
  Like some truant bees at play.

Through the blooming groves we rustle,
  Kissing every bud we pass,—
As we did it in the bustle,
  Scarcely knowing how it was.

Down the glen, across the mountain,
  O'er the yellow heath we roam,
Whirling round about the fountain,
  Till its little breakers foam.

Bending down and weeping willows,
  While our vesper hymn we sigh;
Then unto our rosy pillows
  On our weary wings we hie.

There of idlenesses dreaming,
  Scarce from waking we refrain,
Moments long as ages deeming
  Till we 're at our play again.
                    GEORGE DARLEY.

www.ingramcontent.com/pod-product-compliance
Lightning Source LLC
Chambersburg PA
CBHW031110020726
47495CB00007B/2133